To my deep love of watermelon-flavored Jolly Rancher lollipops and fear of wax figures.

I never thought I'd find a way to write these into a book... yet here we are.

SCOPAESTHESIA

BESTSELLING AUTHOR
A.L. WOODS

ALSO BY A.L. WOODS

THE REFLECTIONS TRILOGY

MIRRORS

SHATTERED

AWAKE

INTO THE STORM SERIES

RAIN

AFTER RAIN

STANDALONES

VERITAS

LIES

IN SECRET WE SIN SERIES

TOXIC

ADRENALINE

SCOPAESTHESIA

PLAYLIST

"My Own Summer (Shove It)" – Deftones
"Embrace" — Ludovico Technique
"A Match Into Water" — Pierce The Veil
"Black No. 1 (Little Miss Scare -All)" — Type O Negative
"Romance" — Varials
"Hickory Creek" — Whitechapel

Scan this code to access the playlist on Spotify

FOREWORD

Scopaesthesia is book #1.5 in the *In Secret We Sin* series and was previously available in the *Phobia: Dark Romance Anthology.*

It can be read as a standalone, but it is best enjoyed as an accompaniment to *Adrenaline,* book one in the series.

Focusing strongly on psychological elements, it contains situations and themes that may be disturbing, including the exploration of automatonophobia—fear of human-like figures—voyeurism, exhibitionism, breeding kink, food play, and graphic mentions of violence.

While the story can be fully enjoyed as a standalone, it ends in a new mystery as it serves as a building block for book two and three in the series.

Reader discretion is advised.

CHAPTER ONE

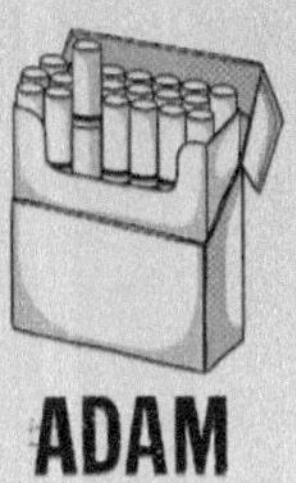

The urgent drumming of Deftones "My Own Summer" vibrated in the cabin of the idling car. I brought the cigarette pinched between my thumb and forefinger to my lips, taking a long pull, expelling the smoke from the corner of my mouth.

My eyes hooded as I studied the tiny figure in the passenger seat of the car, bobbing her head to the music.

My wife, Katrina, was five-foot-nothing. I could practically wrap my hand around her wrist twice and throw her over my shoulder just because I could. She liked the end result of that, anyway.

It would be easy enough to lose her in a sea of average-height people if she didn't change her hair color every couple of weeks. She stood out. Right now, she was sporting a brilliant shade of pumpkin.

The locks were cut into layers she'd done herself, framing her heart-shaped face, ending a little below her exposed collarbones under the sweetheart neckline of her dress. The color was fitting, given we were days away from Halloween. She reached up and tucked the left side behind her ear, revealing her mostly relaxed profile. Her deep red lips stretched over a lollipop. Every so often, she'd torture me and drag it against her extended tongue in a prolonged manner, stopping to examine her progress on the hard candy before slipping it past her lips again. I'd accuse her of trying to start something, but I knew better. My response to her was pheromones, biology, and unadulterated fucking obsession. All she'd ever had to do was exist.

Katrina flitted her made-up warm, honey-brown gaze my way. Sooty, lush false lashes nearly touching her full, feathery brows she'd filled in. Where her older siblings had more classically European features, she had always reminded me of an anime character.

"He's taking *forever*," she whined, projecting her voice out to me over the music, her eyes flicking to the imposing Victorian house on a hill we parked in front of. There wasn't a single light on in the place save for illuminated satin black angle shades curved in front of a rusted antique brass sign reading *Rockchapel Funeral Home*, but I knew he was in there.

Plotting something. I could sense it like a sizzle in the thick air promising rain.

My brother, Vince—not by blood—lived and worked here with his uncle Alek, who owned the funeral home. Katrina called V ten minutes ago to let him know we were here, and he'd grunted at her with acknowledgment before hanging up.

No idea why he couldn't drive himself to the Halloween attraction we were attending tonight, hosted at the local wax museum, but whatever.

Frankly, he could take all fucking long if he wanted to. Every minute he took made my wife a little more fidgety, and I enjoyed watching her get hot and bothered, even if it was from restlessness.

You would think that after six months of being able to call her my wife, some of the allure would have faded by now, but no.

Somehow, I grew more consumed by her as the days stretched into weeks, and weeks into months. How could I not be?

I'd waited four years to get her back. Gone through hell and back just to call her mine again.

Nearly lost her permanently, too.

Death tended to put things into perspective. I knew that firsthand.

That was why I hadn't spared a moment sliding the simple thin rose gold band with a cathedral setting for the moss agate stone and two tiny diamonds on her ring finger, followed by the plain band seated under it.

I'd wanted something understated on her dainty, slender fingers. Something that wouldn't impede her part-time work as a construction supervisor for her family's house-flipping business when she wasn't at school where she was working on her Associate in Architectural and Civil Science Engineering Technology. Something she'd never want to take off.

Not that I'd let her do the latter.

I'd crazy glue it back on her.

I'd tattooed her name across my fingers just so the world knew who I belonged to, too.

I offered her a noncommittal shrug, canting my head. While it was unusual for Vince to take his sweet ass time, he was unusual, period.

Which wasn't saying much coming from me.

My brothers and I weren't exactly the embodiment of calm and normalcy. Our criminal records preceded us around our tiny little town, after all.

Rockchapel—or *Rotchapel* as we locals knew it—was a former tourist town in Massachusetts, bordering Rhode Island.

Seventeen years ago, the local amusement park—Elara Park— became the site of a scandal so great, it permanently mired our town in death and changed my life irrevocably.

A story for another time.

The point was, our town, and its inhabitants, were a little fucking odd. It was rare for anyone to leave, and those who did left with nothing more than the clothes on their backs and a few worldly possessions. Our real estate wasn't worth shit, and the amenities were bar to none. Tourism hadn't been booming here since the golden era in the seventies and eighties. Our version of entertainment, save for the museum and a few local watering holes, was working our way through a steady stream of easy girls we traded like Pokémon cards until we were bored, then our attention shifted to the drugs we could readily get our hands on.

Of course, that had changed for me since I'd gotten myself a wife who would have clawed my fucking eyes out if I so much as turned my head in someone else's direction.

Not that I was interested. She kept my hands full.

Sometimes, it surprised me she'd agreed to move here. Then again, I supposed the architecture of our town appealed to her preservationist tendencies.

Our local government and historical society made it impossible to change anything. Our homes and edifices were a hodgepodge of Gothic revival brick houses and carpenter Gothic homes laden with gingerbread trim and steep gables complimented by bargeboards on the edges. Wrought iron fences lined wide lots and tall ornamental trees, now naked and dormant, canopied the redbrick paved streets.

Katrina said the vibe of the town reminded her of the survival-horror video game *Silent Hill.*

She fit right in.

Katrina's head fell back against her seat, her lips vibrating with the exasperate raspberry she blew out. She lifted her black Doc Marten clad feet to the dash, her gray knit socks bunching over the edge of her boots. My eyes traipsed up the length of her long, lean legs, inspecting the hemline of her army-green plaid-print lace-trim dress bunched at the apex of her thigh and hip, giving me an eyeful of the winding floral and compass tattoo hugging around the curve of her thigh.

My teeth ached with the urge to bite her there.

She kept her attention on the house, swiping her tongue along the sugar that had gathered on her lips despite the lipstick. The gesture sent a flood of desire swelling in my cock, and I parted my legs a little wider to accommodate the growth in my gray joggers, drawing a tight breath through my nose.

I needed to get back into that car.

Taking a final drag on my cigarette, I dropped it to the ground, crushing it under my black Converses. The cold air made my nose run, and I rubbed my hands together to warm them. In about thirty seconds, they were going to be between her thighs and she was going to squeal with protest like she did every night when I came into the house from the garage where I did custom woodwork and I slid my hands up her shirt to palm her barely there breasts or cup her hot pussy.

Consider it my small act of service.

I was reaching for the door handle when the click of the locks engaging hit my ears. I tapered my eyes at her, my heart picking up speed at the flash of her mischievous smile.

Turning down the music, she leaned back in her seat, running the pad of her finger along the unlock button. "What do you say?" she asked, her proud neck elongating.

Bracing a hand against the roof of the car, I inclined my head, speaking into the gap in the window. "*Now*." The threat rumbled in the back of my throat, the surge of blood rushing to both heads.

God, I loved it when she got like this.

Katrina pursed her bee-stung lips with thought, drumming the lollipop against them. "Mm, nope. That's not it." She flexed her legs, the tips of her boots pointing toward the house, the muscles in her calves tightening. Stretching one arm overhead, her tiny breasts pushed against the dress, the folds of her stolen denim jacket opening. Her alert, pierced nipples strained against the flimsy material, my braced hand drumming against the roof.

"Open the door, Little Rabbit."

She flashed me a grin, her longer central incisors like those of a rabbit, revealing themselves to me. A long time ago, she'd admitted to being self-conscious about her teeth. But I loved Katrina's teeth.

I loved that she hogged the blanket in bed, routinely left her empty shampoo bottles in the shower, and would sooner live out of a laundry basket than put her clean clothes away.

I loved her ever-changing hair, the playfulness in her eyes and the adrenaline junky she never kept contained with me.

I loved that despite the hell my brothers and I put through her, the resentment I'd hidden behind to deny her my love, she had loved me anyway.

She chose me.

She was *my* wife, mine to hold, to fuck, and to love.

Which was what I suspected she wanted to hear. My eyes molted, heat spreading through me despite the frigid October chill as she waited patiently, teasing the lock button with the pad of her finger. "I love you."

Katrina craned her head, holding a hand to her ear. "What was that?"

She was going to get it. Any stiffer and I was going to bust clean through the seam of these pants.

"I love you."

Her features screwed up, and she fought to keep the smile in check, pursing her lips. "Hm?"

"I love you!" I shouted, pounding my open palm against the roof of the car, the blow spreading an ache through my fingers.

"*Oh,*" she crooned, dropping her legs to the car floor, and inclining back in her seat. "No need to shout, husband." My chest puffed. I fucking loved when she called me that. She waved a hand at me with a flourish. "Access granted."

I jerked the driver's door open as soon as the lock disengaged, her high-pitched squeal eating up the transient silence as the song changed and "A Match Into Water" by Pierce the Veil played from the auxiliary cable hooked to her iPod. Recognizing the gravity of her screw up, the hand not holding the lollipop shot for the seatbelt release, trying to buy her freedom. But she would never escape me.

Not in this lifetime or the next one.

Ever.

I trapped her against the seat, caging her body with mine when I crossed the middle console. Lowering my face to hers, her sugary exhales fanned my lips with warmth. "And where do you think you're going, hm?" I questioned, brushing my nose against hers.

Katrina's soft whimper made my cock throb for her attention.

She attempted to close the distance with her lips, but I jerked my head back, keeping her body fixed in place. Her brows crushed together, her lids growing heavy. "Kiss me," she demanded, breathless.

"What's the magic word?"

"*Now*," she mocked, running her upper teeth along her bottom lip, her throat bobbing with a swallow. I reached for the hand holding her lollipop, guiding it to my mouth. The artificial flavor of watermelon danced on my tastebuds, my eyes holding hers as I swirled my tongue along it. Her intakes hitched, her thighs finding each other under me, clenching.

"Please," she whispered, the vowels in the word twisting into a desperate beg.

Releasing the lollipop, I wet my lips, never breaking eye contact. "Please, what?" I rasped, touching my cold nose to her warmer one, circling the thin hoop of her septum piercing. Her lips parted, her pupils dilating just a little under my appraisal. As the silence stretched between us, she rubbed her lips together with anticipation and I spotted the fight in her limbs dissipating, her neck arching with surrender.

She wasn't just interested in kissing me anymore. "Please touch me," she said, confirming my suspicions.

"Where?" I questioned, dropping my head to the sensitive spot under her ear, her rose garden perfume wafting into my nose. At her silence, I fitted my lips against her pulse. "Here?" Goosebumps bloomed across her skin, her shiver quaking her slender frame.

"Or…?" I continued my descent down her exposed collarbone, my teeth sliding along the protruding bone. Her heartbeat pounded, reverberating against my mouth as I teased the sweetheart neckline of her dress with the tip of my nose. Sandwiching the neckline of the dress between my teeth, I peeled it over the curve of her left tit, her stiff pierced nipple puckered in offering for me. Opening my mouth wide, I vacuumed the swell into my mouth, my teeth brandishing the soft skin, my tongue laving at the hardened point and barbell.

"Fuck," she cried out, her impatient hips levitating off the seat.

Grinning against her tit, I released it from the torturous confines of my mouth. "I bet you'd like that, wouldn't you?" I asked, my voice husky. "You'd like nothing more than for me to fuck you with the threat of getting caught, right?"

It wouldn't be the first time and I'd be a liar if I didn't admit it was one of my kinks of choice, too. I loved taking her anywhere the chance of us being caught existed. I loved showing her off to the world, so they knew who she belonged to.

Katrina's breaths quickened, her grip on the lollipop almost going completely slack. An idea came to mind, and I guided the lollipop to my mouth again, freeing her of the responsibility.

"Spread your legs," I urged around the candy, hiking the material of her dress up higher. She shifted in her seat, her legs parting, offering me a flash of her black bikini style underwear with the most deceptive bow detailing the front against a splash of white polka dots.

Innocent in a way she absolutely wasn't.

I could smell the heady need wafting off her pussy. Bringing a cold, blunt finger to the damp spot of her panties, her sharp gasp twisted into a whimper as I teased her, trailing my finger from the pulsating heat of her swollen lips up to the sensitive nub of flesh.

"What are you going to do the next time I try to get to you?"

"Lock you out," she confirmed, sounding every bit as fucking sultry as she looked.

"That's right." Just the way I wanted it. The hunt. "But it's not going to matter, is it?" I probed, pressing my impossibly hard cock against her belly, rutting against her slowly. "'Cause you can't stay away from me."

"And you can't stay away from me."

"That's right, baby," I growled out. "I can't stay away from you. You can lock every single door you want. You can run and hide, but I'll always find you because you're mine, and I'm yours."

"You're mine, and I'm yours," she echoed, her legs straining wider, the muscles in her thighs flexing. The gesture tested the strength of her thin panties, the fabric settling between her engorged labia, swollen with need. I hooked a finger under the soaked material, tugging it to the right, her eyes rolling up to the cabin of her Jeep.

"Eyes on me," I reminded.

Short of me taking her from behind, or me pining her head to the mattress, I always wanted the heat of her eyes locked on mine, to feel the magnitude of our connection because we were fucking transcendental.

I extended my tongue, swiping it along the lollipop on both sides until it shimmered. Katrina's eyes distended, and I watched her fight the urge to track the lollipop as I lowered it between us, finding her clit.

She jumped at the contact, her hands finding purchase on my biceps, her expel of breath leaving her in a shocked huff. I circled her clit with the tip, coaxing each shaky exhale out of her, her eyes fighting to stay open. The lollipop slid downward, gathering her arousal on the sugary piece of heaven. Bringing it back between us, her grip on me tightened as I popped the lollipop into my mouth and bit down on it, the sweet candy giving away readily under the pressure, earning the flaring of her eyes as I savored my favorite taste.

Her.

If I could preserve the taste of her pussy in a candy form so I could have her full-bodied sweet-and-earthy flavor playing on my tongue all day, I would.

Discarding the candy stick to the emptied cup holder, I propped all of my weight on my left hand, pulling myself closer to her so I could fit my right hand between her legs. Her back bowed a little as my deft fingers ambled up the inside of her thigh, her ardent gaze locked on mine over the bridge of her nose.

My knuckles brushed along the pleat of her pussy and her sharp sigh pushed a shot of lust into my veins that felt like pure epinephrine, knocking air momentarily out of my lungs, making my head spin. She was my personal adrenaline rush and every frantic, needy sound she made pulled me deeper into her. I stroked along her twice before turning my hand, my middle finger swiping along her, collecting her body's honey along my finger.

A musical cry lodged itself in her throat when I tunneled my finger forward, her tight, warm channel stretching along the invasion, inch by delicious inch, and squeezing around me. My heart pounded in my chest as my thoughts raced out of control and I had to remind myself to concentrate.

I wanted to hook her legs over the bend of my elbows and fuck her into her car until we broke the suspension, or worse.

I wanted our birth control to fail so we could finally start our family and we could have a half dozen facsimiles of us running around our house.

I just wanted her. All of her. How ever I could have her, forever.

Katrina squirmed under me when I drew my finger back out. Her right hand shot to the window, her fingers splayed as my pointer finger joined my left finger, thrusting forward in search of that toe-curling, ecstasy-inducing place.

"Adam, Adam, Adam!" she chanted my name, her body bucking under me.

Bingo.

Her hips rocked forward, my thumb seating against her clit, as I found a rhythm, pumping my fingers in and out of her, maintaining the motion of my massaging thumb. The pinched concentration on her face told me she was close, her resolve and focus straining. Heat spread from my groin, tingling in my limbs. Precum leaked from the crown of my cock, sticking and chafing the inside of my boxer briefs while sweat cooled my spine as my slow rocking turned into gyrating grinding against her, growing more urgent with every passing second as her inner muscles quivered in warning around my fingers.

But the burst of her release wouldn't come in time.

From the corner of my eye, a towering shadow fell across the hood of the car and before either of us could react, a fist pounded against the driver's side window. Katrina jolted, the spell of the moment breaking, her defensive reflexes forcing a hand to shoot for the lock on the door again as she looked in the rearview mirror.

She sagged in a combination of relief and annoyance when she realized who was rounding the car.

"Took him long enough," she mumbled.

The back door opened, a gust of fall wind ushering in Vince's woody bergamot cologne and the traces of cigarettes still on his skin as he settled in the seat behind her. Looking tickled fucking pink, he slammed the door shut, the SUV rocking.

Stroking his thumb along his bottom lip, Vince's amusement

curved his mouth into a sinister simper, his eyes half-hooded. "Don't let me stop you," he murmured, that punchable unrelenting, hard jaw tightening. "By all means, continue."

He stretched an arm over the back seat, his parted knees digging into Katrina's seat, resulting in her scowl. His cruel dark gaze found mine in the gap of her headrest, and his thick brows relaxed. "I know how much you like it when you have an audience."

Katrina's legs clamped shut, her lips rolling together as the crimson stain of humiliation spread up the column of her creamy neck.

I tapered my eyes at him.

There was a very fine line between knowing you were being watched from the shadows and an entirely different thing having your audience announce themselves and act smug about it.

I bent my head her way, feathering my lips against hers, finally kissing her. She dissolved under me, her left hand bracketing my cheek, her soft sigh sinking into my bones. Inching her head back a little, she brushed the tip of her nose against mine, communicating she was okay.

Slowly, I slid my fingers from inside of her, the cold draft chilling my slick fingers. "Open," I instructed.

The blush returned, heating her cheeks, beads of sweat shining against her hairline. Her pillowy lips parted, and I coaxed my fingers inside of her mouth. I watched as her cheeks hollowed out and she licked them clean for me, my cock protesting in my joggers.

Vince had the worst timing.

"We'll finish this later," I told her under my breath, adjusting myself with my free hand.

She could be sure about that.

CHAPTER TWO

KATRINA

There was an excited energy permeating through the air as we clambered out of my Jeep, the laughter and hubbub of chatter filling the night. I was lifting my booted foot to the curb when I got hauled into a stiff, trim body, warm lips that betrayed the rest of him fitting against my forehead.

Vince was as warm as a corpse on a good day, but our relationship was unique.

Or as unique as the source of the growl to my left would permit.

"Hands. Off. Now," Adam commanded, his lilt a combination of Massachusetts and Rhode Island with a sharp edge to it that made my skin prickle and the space between my legs pulsate with a starved ache.

Vince chuckled against me, shoving me gently in Adam's direction. "Off you go, before he takes my head off for funsies."

My husband was… um, *possessive*, to say the very least, but I supposed he had his reasons.

After all, I'd been with Vince.

I paused, ruminating for a moment. And Gabriel.

Slouching into the neckline of my coat, I blew out a sigh. And Maxwell.

Under ordinary circumstances, I might have felt bad about it, but because of those experiences with them, Adam and I were what we were.

Inseparable.

If it hadn't been for the three of them and their maniacal puppeteering, my husband might not have gotten his head out of his ass, and I might have still been the frightened little rabbit, too afraid to take up space in the world.

To ask for what she wanted, to be brave, and to be a proverbial wolf.

Unstoppable.

So no, I wasn't ashamed I'd fucked my husband's best friends, his brothers. I refused to be burdened by my history with them anymore than my guilt of what I'd done to my husband a lifetime ago.

We'd needed to fall apart to come back together again, to break into a dozen pieces so we could fill the cracks between us with gold and create something new, something that was ours. It didn't matter that the outside world would never understand us, that they would treat it as something lewd and dirty. We didn't need them to disentangle it because the story was ours and ours alone.

I shored up to Adam's body, tucking myself under his armpit, wrapping an arm around his waist. "It was just a hug," I soothed, tracing the stitching on his black-and-white varsity jacket.

"To *you*," he muttered, his impenetrable hazel stare burning with murder as he regarded Vince. "Not to him." The mean skull tattooing Adam's neck shifted with his swallow, his head pitching a little to the right.

Vince held his hands up, offering my husband a guilty look. "True. She was one of my favorite fucks," he taunted.

Adam bared his teeth, taking a threatening step forward. The lock of my arm around his waist struggled to keep him in place.

"Vincent," I chastised, shooting him an imploring look over my shoulder. "Cut it out."

He was such a shit disturber. I knew he was teasing. While Adam had accepted as best as he could what had gone down between his friends and me, he didn't like the reminder or having it slung back in his face.

We'd had one extensive discussion about it shortly before we'd gotten married and then archived it in the "avoid at all costs" filing cabinet.

Which mostly worked, and I hoped when there came a time when his brothers found partners of their own, that they too could wrap their heads around it.

Maxwell had been determined to pretend what happened between us was nothing more than a terrible fever dream equivalent to him stepping outside of the house wearing H&M over his usual sell-an-organ high-end apparel. Not all of us had older sisters with closets they could shop in.

Gabriel still gave me that lost puppy lovestruck look which made me feel guilty, but I knew at his core, I wasn't who he was longing for.

And Vince made a point of never wasting a single moment to get under Adam's skin about it, telling me while examining his short fingernails, *"The threat of losing you again to one of us makes the sex better, doesn't it?"* As though this was his form of altruism, and he was doing us a public service.

All this was to say we knew none of them would ever act on it again. That the chapter was permanently sealed shut and encased six feet in the ground in a concrete coffin.

I pushed my nose into Adam's side, inhaling him. Sandalwood and ginger took the edge off the moment, and I propped my chin against his ribcage, observing his tense profile, his jaw as stiff as granite. "C'mon, grumpy."

Adam's glare left Vince's, scowling down at me. He drew in his naturally hollowed-out cheeks, sandwiching the skin between his molars. The streetlight caught on the hoop fed through his flared right nostril. "I'm *not* grumpy."

Yeah, yeah. And they hadn't done worse things than what they'd gone to jail for.

I framed my hands on his stubbled cheeks, savoring the rasp against my palms while searching his eyes. "You're right," I observed lowly. "You're horny. Which is worse."

Adam with blue balls was a hazard to himself.

He lifted a daring brow at me, the frustration vanishing from the mossy green-brown orbs, heat taking over. Without warning, his tattooed hand closed around the back of my neck, his fingers shoving through my hair, forcing me onto the tips of my toes to close the distance. It was like the rest of the world faded away around us, his stare holding my own. The pleat of his lips fitted against mine, his hands keeping me pinned against him, refusing to allow me to come up for air or to ease the ache in my trembling, overextended toes. His teeth nipped at my bottom lip with a promise, and he released his hold on the back of my neck, setting me flat on my feet again.

Linking my fingers with his, I gave him a reassuring squeeze, following his long strides as he led me toward a massive, two-story stone structure, separate from the rows of historical facades lining the one-way street. Weather-beaten gargoyles fringed the ornate, carved tracery of the roofline, guarding the edifice. The roof sloped into a nave, flying buttresses on either end of the building, and a stained-glass wheel window reflected blue and red light to the street below. It looked like it had once been a theater of some sort.

God, I loved this town and its buildings.

Beneath the window was an out-of-place marquee jutting out, reading *Wagner Wax Museum and Other Oddities.*

Excitement kicked my pulse to life as we neared the clusters of people standing outside of the building, huddled in tight groups to stave off the chill. The fall air was crisp and sharp, and it tickled my nose, my breaths leaving my mouth in a cloud of steamy vapors.

From beyond the double glass doors—the most modern feature on the structure—industrial Gothic metal pounded, the glow of dim lighting illuminating the vestibule.

I'd never visited the museum before, but I knew of its existence. I didn't see the appeal of wax figures, though I could appreciate the time that went into any art form, no matter how creepy it was.

Online, I'd read that in late September, it transformed from its usual wax figure lineup to a Chamber of Horrors. Grizzly crime scene recreations, homage to serial killers—real and fictional—and replica medieval torture devices were on display. They converted gallery rooms into mazes, and they peppered scare actors between the figures, making it impossible to discern who was real and who wasn't. Maybe you'd get scared out in the open with a crowd to bleed into, or perhaps you'd find yourself lost within the labyrinths while the threat of someone who knew the museum like the back of their hand charged after you.

I wasn't sure how much I liked the latter. A nervous shiver crawled up my spine, my stomach flipping at the threat. I was an adrenaline junkie, sure, and that came with a certain level of love for the fear of the unknown, but it was a whole other beast when you were pursued by someone who wanted to scare you for no other reason but because they were being paid to do so.

It lacked authenticity, so it was going to be an interesting night.

Joining the long queue, I leaned against Adam, trying to warm up. Painful goosebumps stretched along the stretch of my exposed legs, my toes curling into my boots. His fingers splayed on my back, swishing back and forth, trying to keep me warm. Stealing a peek at Vince, I studied the pensive set of his jaw and slight bend in his brows as though he were concentrating more than usual. Something told me it wasn't because he couldn't wait to get inside the building.

"Why did you want a ride?" I asked, our footfalls falling into an unintentional synchronization as we moved with the cue closer to the building.

"So he could piss me off," Adam muttered, keeping his attention pointed straight ahead.

Vince's brittle laugh rumbled in his chest as he pulled a shiny red apple out of his jacket's interior pocket, tossing it in the air and catching it with ease. He almost always had an apple on him or within reach. "You flatter me."

That wasn't exactly an answer, though.

Adam flipped him the bird, clearly not caring what his reason was.

But I did. Rockchapel wasn't particularly big to begin with, occupying only fifteen miles. Vince lived only five minutes away and going to pick him up had required us to make a slight detour.

He could have walked if he didn't feel like driving tonight.

Suspicion spiked in my veins, and I narrowed my focus on Vince, really taking him in. He never did anything without a reason. So, what the hell was he up to?

His styled, raven-black hair pushed off his forehead, his thick brows at ease over his equally dark, brown-eyed gaze. Despite the faint traces of aftershave on his skin, I could already see the sprouting of regrowth dusting his jaw. Now that he knew I was paying attention, he wasn't going to give me anything to run with. Well, almost nothing. The formation of a smirk touched his lips for the briefest moment before it vanished.

Vince was as tall as a renaissance statue. He had a whole foot and then some over me and always had to incline his frame to meet mine, my head landing a little under his pec. The black waffle-knit Henley he donned stretched over his frame like saran wrap, his free hand tucked into the pocket of his black zip-front bomber jacket.

He constantly dressed like he was attending a funeral, and I supposed it was fitting, given his family's line of business. Vince had been embalming bodies well before he could even get his learner's permit. It was in his blood.

Adam was the shortest of his brothers at five-eleven, but I'd always felt his energy took up the most space. It was larger than life, overshadowing his friends somehow.

Redirecting my attention forward, I brushed my fingers along Adam's black wedding band, his stiff inked fingers constricting around mine. He twisted the hoop fed through his right nostril, his eyes tracking the throngs of people. He was always surveying people, hunting for an anomaly. The only time he looked completely at ease was the fleeting times he entered a deep sleep. But even then, some-times his nightmares caught up with him.

By contrast to Vince's attire, my husband was a whatever was clean kind of guy. He had an arsenal of plaid shirts I frequently stole. While he normally wore distressed jeans with intentional holes in them and frays around the knees, today, he'd opted for joggers that were tight around his calves and did little to disguise what was sheathed beyond the fabric. It was sweatpants season and Adam in joggers turned him into a walking thirst trap. The autumnal breeze toyed with the strings of his hoodie under his jacket, and the scuffs on his Converses illuminated under the glow of the streetlights. He had the kind of face you couldn't help but study—squared jaw peppered in three-day-old scruff, the same shade as his mahogany hair, hollowed cheeks, and hazel eyes fringed by dark lashes.

"I like it when you eye fuck me," he began under his breath, rubbing his thinner top lip into his bottom. "But if you don't stop, we're not going to make it in there."

Vince snorted behind us. So much for Adam's attempt at discretion.

I tipped my head down, heat rising to my cheeks.

The line flowed quickly, and before I knew it, we were approaching the box office. When the hyper teenage girls barreled away from the box office, Adam approached, towing me gently with him. He shoved a hand through his shock of mahogany hair, and the nervous elfin of a woman behind the plexiglass shrunk in her seat, cowering.

Her brassy, copper hair frizzed around her forehead; the rest pulled back in a messy, thick braid sloped over the knitted sweater.

"Two," Adam said.

The girl nodded, punching something into the computer.

"*Three*," I corrected.

My husband wasn't amnesiac, but he was an asshole.

He swung his gaze my way, his jaw popping with annoyance. He wasn't really not going to pay for Vince, was he?

His scowl softened just a little when I kicked my chin up at him, crossing my arms over my chest, the gesture pushing my tiny breasts upward. His eyes crinkled in the corners with amusement, and he drove his thumb behind him. "I'm not paying for him."

I dropped my arms, jabbing a finger in the center of his chest. "Don't be an ass, Adam."

We didn't have that kind of relationship with our family. We took care of each other and didn't split hairs about who owed who what.

Vince's shadow fell upon the plexiglass. "I don't need him to pay for me. I'm not staying," he announced, his voice cold and devoid of any emotion.

Huh? Then why the hell had he come?

I tracked his hand as he brought the apple to his mouth. He jutted his chin at her. "Call your boss, Baby Fischer."

Adam lifted a questioning brow at the demand.

The girl behind the box office's plexiglass flinched as though Vince had struck her when his teeth penetrated the flesh, her spine growing ramrod straight.

I felt bad for her, even if it seemed like he knew her. Adam let out a pitiful sigh through his nose, his earlier annoyance long gone. Vince had that effect on people. I offered her an apologetic smile, but she didn't look my way. Her frightened brown eyes lowered toward the desk, her frame curving in on itself like she wanted to disappear.

It was strange how out of sorts she seemed here. Like she was employed here against her will, or didn't want to be here at all.

Vincent wasn't helping matters as he loomed closer to the plexiglass, staring down at her like she was a toy left for his entertainment… or his prey.

When she didn't acknowledge him, he ran a finger against the barrier, the acrylic squeaking under his motion. She cowed deeper in her seat, but she didn't dare look up at him. Not that I blamed her.

He was taunting her.

"Vincent," I scolded, taking pity on the scared girl, flicking my eyes between my husband and his best friend. "Quit it."

Adam let out a snort.

I lifted my chin at him. "That goes for you, too. Neither of you have any manners."

Sometimes, I felt like a mother hen, nitpicking at the guys to be polite. It was like they didn't know how to behave in public. They leaned into their pack and delinquent mentality a bit too much, and it was unsettling for people.

Hell, it used to scare the shit out of me.

"Don't talk to me about manners, Little Rabbit," Vince rebutted, with his mouth full, swallowing. Losing interest in the girl behind the glass, he studied the apple, lifting his obsidian eyes to me. "Didn't stop you from getting finger fucked in front of my house, right?" he accused, confirming what I'd already suspected. Vince had been lurking around the car much longer than he had announced himself. He'd intentionally waited until he knew my climax was close, reading my body's tells like a book.

I gaped at him, mortified. But it was nothing compared to the girl— Baby Fischer, whatever her name was—who looked like she wanted to die on the spot from secondhand embarrassment.

"What did I tell you about calling her that?" Adam challenged darkly, his eyes thinning. He hated anyone else calling me by that nickname. It was only his to use now. "Or watching?"

Vince pursed his lips, blowing him an antagonistic kiss. "But that's what you kids love."

I rolled my eyes heavenward. It wasn't the same, and he knew it. Puffing air up into my full fringe, the bright orange strands fluttered. "It's a stupid nickname." I didn't need the constant reminder that I had bad teeth.

Adam turned around, his upper lip curving back.

He loved my teeth. He reminded me daily.

"You're going to pay for that," he warned me, running his fingers back and forth along his lips with thought. The space between us crackled with the predatory charge, and my body hummed to life again, my core clenching around nothing.

I shot him a heated smile, my insecurities melting away. "I can't wait."

Adam never looked away as he tugged his wallet out of his pocket and pulled out the amount needed for our admission—only for two, living up to his word. He fed it in the opening in the plexiglass, and with quaking, quick hands, the anxious girl punched in the total and offered him his change and our tickets. She was reaching for the phone, when a shadow fell upon her, shrinking the box office. A man, no older than Adam or Vince, lingered behind her, his hand swallowing hers when it bolted over her clutch on the phone.

She looked shellshocked, completely frozen in place, like her soul had left her body.

But he… he looked at her like Adam looked at me. His lips moved, murmuring something to her.

Her stare followed the slope of an arm attached to the man who dressed like he shopped where Vince did—*Dead People R' Us*—and hadn't seen the sun for at least six months. He donned black jeans and a black dress shirt a size too small around his biceps, rolled up to his elbows. His equally black hair was short and cropped to his scalp, and the bright green veins in his defined forearm flexed from where he gripped her.

Neither of them acknowledged us.

For a split second, it seemed like we were intruding on whatever was going on between them until he extracted his hand from hers and straightened, his spine uncoiling.

What was in the water in Rockchapel? Another giant was in our midst.

The softness in his expression evacuated, and the geodes of his gray, unyielding eyes turned hard when he regarded Vince. "Markov," he said flatly, addressing Vince by his last name.

Was this why Vince tagged along with us?

Vince flicked his eyes from the girl back to the man, newfound interest erasing his stony expression. His boredom returned as he examined the mostly eaten apple. "Wagner."

Wagner. He must own the museum or be related to the owners.

While Vince's voice remained devoid of amusement, to the untrained ear, they didn't hear what Adam and I did.

He was up to no good, and whatever he'd witnessed between the girl behind the till and Wagner, he was keeping in his back pocket for a rainy day.

Wagner gestured with his head for Vince to follow. Nodding, Vince took a last bite from his apple, depositing the core on the edge of the box office for someone else to clean up after him.

I sighed.

"Asshole," Wagner muttered, leading him through a side door and disappearing from our line of sight.

Clearing his throat, Adam slung an arm over my shoulders, but I detected the lingering uneasy tension in his body. He didn't trust Vince. That made two of us. "C'mon. Let's go get the shit scared out of us."

I smiled into his side, trying to push the Vince and Wagner interaction out of my mind. There was only one person getting scared tonight, and I knew it was me.

CHAPTER THREE

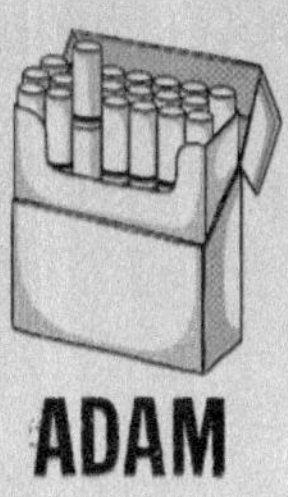

"I wonder what Vince is up to," Katrina said, her hand linked to mine.

I didn't reply. I'd rather not know what Vince was up to. It was better for everyone.

At my silence, she posed another question, her attention trained on the glass display case under bright picture lights we stopped in front of. "Do you know them?"

We were on the main floor of the museum, having cleared the vestibule, and handed our tickets to the waiting attendants at the door. They donned black T-shirts with the museum's logo on the breast.

The main floor of the museum had a checkered marble floor pattern, the harsh black-and-white colors softened under the ornate ballroom chandelier with tawny bulbs overhead. There was a deep, blood-red carpet runner leading to a wooden flight of bifurcated staircase that belonged in a mansion and not in a museum.

Then again, the structure had once belonged to one of the Rockchapel Founding Families two hundred years ago—a bunch of Puritans with a moral compass the size of Mother Teresa's patience. So, it fit that the structure had over-the-top features.

Nothing but the best for the wealthy.

Insert eye roll here.

I examined the wooden buttress suspended over the foot of the stairs; it supported the overhead balcony. Elaborate newel posts bled into smooth handrails, and the balusters featured ornamental cast-iron round posts gleaming under the chandelier. The glow of carved pumpkins cast haunting shadows along the wooden risers, their radiance flickering along people who passed.

The coffered ceilings were at least twenty feet high and painted a deep brown color, the same shade as the walls that somehow didn't shrink the room.

Katrina was in her glory but seemed less impressed with the whole point of the building. I'd nearly barreled into her when I'd led her through a narrow, borderline claustrophobic moulage hallway by the waist and she realized the impressions had belonged to real dead people. The epiphany caused her to come to an abrupt dead stop. Her full lips stretched into a grimace, and her eyes rounding to the size of dinner plates.

I wasn't sure how she was going to fare when we got upstairs, but we'd see.

This had been her idea, not mine.

"Do I know who?" I asked, studying the curve of her profile. Her pert nose wrinkled at the rows of diaphonized animal skeletons in glass jars.

I was confident the animal remains reminded her of a moment in our lives she didn't want to revisit, and I didn't blame her.

I'd give anything to undo all of that for her.

She twisted around to face me, the hem of her dress catching air, picking up over her thighs. "The girl in the box office and Wagner."

I knew who Rhys Wagner was. Regretfully. I rocked my jaw, considering how much to divulge to her. "It's a small town, baby. Everyone knows everyone."

Especially Josephine. The girl had tried her damnedest to remain invisible since the day she had the misfortune of leaving her mother's womb, but it was no use.

Not with Briar as her older sister. She made Vince almost seem perfectly sound of mind because he had a method to his madness and maintained a fucked-up construct of rules he abided by.

Briar had no such limits. She didn't give a shit that Josephine was her kid sister.

All the more reason to torture her and make her pay a penance for something she could have never prevented. Something that wasn't her fault.

"*I* don't know everyone," Katrina reminded, a tiny smile blooming on her pretty lips. I shifted in place. Those lips would look better stretched around my cock and I flicked my eyes around the main floor, searching for an alcove to drag her into. "Give me the tea."

Especially to get her the fuck off this topic.

I scratched the back of my neck. "The prick with the chip on his shoulder is Rhys Wagner. He owns the museum."

Katrina snorted, her lips rolling together like she was fighting the urge to remind me I wasn't exactly the epitome of approachability myself.

Vince, Gabe, and I had gone to high school with Rhys, and he was our age. He barely uttered two words to anyone, communicating only with glares and head nods. Back then, his head remained buried in one of his weird anatomy textbooks while he huddled over a sketchbook, replicating what he was looking at, graphite discoloring his hands while he worked the pencil back and forth, dumping whatever was in his head onto paper.

Pretentious fuck.

Despite that, he had that whole moody-artist vibe going for him that somehow got him as much pussy as it did us. It didn't seem to matter he rarely opened his mouth. He was unwittingly popular, well-liked, and ended up at the same house parties we'd attended. Tall, dark, and broody mysterious bullshit lingering in a corner, waiting for his next meal to come to him. I would have hated him if I hadn't been impressed.

Vince was less amused, making a point of intercepting Rhys's would-be conquests before they could get to him. A wolf outfoxing the hawk.

Gabe took up drawing for two weeks before he decided he didn't need a skill set to pull girls. Which really meant he couldn't even draw stick people straight. His lines were all slanted.

"And the girl?" Katrina prompted.

I hesitated, begging her with my eyes to move on. Shit, I'd listen to her go on another tangent about how she wanted to install an oriel window on our house over having this conversation.

"Adam." She was losing her patience, and this would have been easier if we were at home and I coulda dragged her under me already to distract her, but no.

We had to go outside and do stuff and be active members of society. Her words, not mine.

Ugh.

But I really didn't want to trigger her. I knew talking about Josephine Fischer beyond the superficial stuff could do just that, so I needed to choose my words wisely. "Her name's Josie Fischer."

"Josie Fischer," she echoed, her lips crooking into a slight smile, like she was testing the name out and liked it. "She seems young for him," she added, rocking back and forth on the heels of her boots, looking around the gallery.

Young for who?

Before I could question my nosy little wife, her shoulders punched up to her ears when she noticed the taxidermy animals on display to the left of the glass jars. Her eyes tapered with mistrust on a stuffed Canadian goose. Its thin, elongated black neck craned in her direction, its wings frozen mid-flap, flight feathers proud. Spiky teeth lined the bird's bared tongue from within its fixed open mouth. I'd recalled a story she'd told me about being chased by one as a kid at a family picnic.

Vicious fucks.

"And afraid of him," she added.

Huh? I raised a brow at her.

She tore her stare away from the goose, her head slanting. "They're together, aren't they?" Curiosity rounded her eyes, her bright orange hair slipping over her shoulder. "Josie and Rhys?"

I gave her a clipped shake of my head. Rhys Wagner *with* Baby Fischer? That would fucking be something that would send Briar on another psychotic rampage. Briar had it bad for Rhys. The entire town knew that. I'd never seen someone rebuffed and humiliated so many times over the years, only to come back for more at the next opportunity. Rhys didn't react to much, but anytime Briar sidled up next to him with a flirty smile and cushioned his arm between the tunnel of her tits, he sneered at her and ripped his arm away like she was corrosive matter or downright repulsed him. Briar didn't have a shot in hell. We all could see that, but all it did was fuel her to try harder. She wasn't used to being told "no", and for someone who didn't have the right last name in this town, she often got what she wanted—and got away with it, too.

Even when it came to hurting her sister. People either turned their heads or pretended it hadn't happened at all because of *who* had helped her.

The reminder had my blood boiling all over again. Look, I wasn't exactly the personification of sound mental health or an ardent follower of the Commonwealth of Massachusetts' penal system even if my wife's eldest sister and her husband-to-be were lawyers with enough cop friends to make me yack.

My first foray with the law letting me down was seventeen years ago, when my father was killed.

They called it an accident.

I called it murder and added names to a list.

I'd sought my revenge when the time was right.

We got caught the first time, and that had cost Vince and me five years of our lives.

But the second time?

I fought back the smile.

Justice served. No cop was ever going to do that. No detective gave a shit when you cried in front of him and recalled what you'd seen. He offered you a can of store brand cola, a stale cookie, and asked you to repeat your story again with bored eyes.

I believed if you didn't fit the bill of what a cop decided a victim should look like; you would never get your justice. It hadn't mattered that I'd been a kid.

But if you looked like the perfect criminal, if you had a motive— well, your life was going to be a living hell. Cops had fucked me. So I learned.

I couldn't wrap my head around how anyone could do that to their kid sister. How anyone could have tried to ignore it happened at all. I would have razed this entire fucking town if anyone so much as breathed in my kid sister Saorise's direction the wrong way.

Josephine was harmless, timid and scared on a good day. Always had been. Saoirse had tried to befriend her for years, but Josie avoided her the way she avoided everyone.

Kind of like Rhys did. Only Rhys had looks going for him and Josie was… forgettable.

"Maybe if I'd tried harder to be her friend, it wouldn't have happened," Saoirse had told me once. *"Maybe I could have stopped it."* My sister couldn't have stopped it, because when someone was sick enough to want to do that to you, all they needed was a little patience and an opportunity.

Rolling out my tense shoulders, I felt the knot shift there and click, followed by a spike of heated adrenaline pushing through my veins.

I didn't make a habit of thinking about Josie because it made me think of every person who'd ever said "no". It forced me to think of Katrina's trauma, the lingering aftermath of it, how I had to be careful not to touch her in a way that had the potential to trigger her.

I could have stopped it had I been there.

So, like Saoirse, I blamed myself every time my wife had a night terror that had her shooting upright in bed, screaming and kicking the blankets away from her. I had scooped her up into my arms countless times when we were in public and someone brushed up against her and she drew in a strained breath and made that face of warning that the onset of a panic attack was nearing.

She'd gotten stronger over the last couple of months, yes, but it hadn't changed how I wished she'd never had to become that way—and that was on me.

"Hm," Katrina hummed out loud, the gesture pulling me out of my dark reverie. I wanted to haul her into me. I wanted to bury my nose against the crook of her neck, to inhale her, and grip her tightly in my embrace and promise to always protect her and keep her from harm.

She stared at me with those cartoony features pulled into a sly grin and a gleam in her honey-brown eyes. Her slender shoulders rose and fell in a shrug. "Well, he likes her."

Clearing my throat, I looked away from her and kept my tone indifferent. "The only thing Rhys likes is himself."

But I knew that wasn't entirely true, either. I'd seen exactly what she'd witnessed, too. He was uncharacteristically gentle with Josie, and it betrayed everything I knew about him.

The question was *why*?

"How old is she?"

"Saoirse's age," I volunteered. Saoirse was twenty-one to my thirty.

She harrumphed. "Too young to be dating an old man."

I narrowed my eyes at her, not missing the jab. "Who you calling old?" There were only five years between us, and it had never been an issue.

Katrina pinched her lips together to keep from laughing, taking a step closer toward the taxidermy animals. I waylaid her before she could get too far, bounding an arm around her slim waist. "I asked you a question."

She leaned against me, the globes of her ass pressing against my stirring cock, her soft sigh mainlining straight to my brain and coaxing out my uncontrolled groan.

Fuck. The breathy sighs and sounds she made could bring me to my knees.

"You, maybe," she taunted under her breath. My cock tented against the seam of my joggers, finding its home against the pleat of her ass cheeks.

We should have stayed home.

Popped in a horror movie if she was so determined to have the shit scared out of her. I could have timed her climaxes with the jump scares, but instead, we were here, and she was torturing me with her come-fuck-me eyes, teasing smiles, and a million fucking questions about Josie and Rhys that I wanted to silence by feeding her my cock.

My mouth found the shell of her ear, and I lowered my voice to stop people nearby from overhearing me. My fingers splayed against her abdomen, pinning her tight against me. "I'm not above placing your hands on that glass," she tracked my eyes to the display case next to us, "bunching your dress over your waist and spanking you until you're begging me to stop or to fuck you in front of these people." She wet her lips at the threat, massaging them together. "Don't push me, Little Rabbit."

She lifted her dilated eyes. "Old. Man," she punctuated under her breath, pulling out of my grasp.

Fucking brat.

Katrina glanced over her shoulder, calling my bluff, and I stroked my jaw, watching the way her hips naturally swayed as she headed for the stairs. She tossed me a playful look over her shoulders. "Coming, husband?"

Oh, I'd be coming alright, and so would she.

"*Coming*, wife."

Bet on it.

CHAPTER FOUR

KATRINA

I'D NEVER SCARED EASILY.

Growing up, I'd made it my life's greatest work to scare my siblings. My older brother, Sean, was the hardest one to scare. I thought that stemmed from being the "man" of the house since our dad died when I was ten to Sean's twenty.

He was always on high alert by extension. Little got past him despite my best efforts.

Maria, the eldest sibling of our brood, was a little easier, and it wasn't because she was clueless but because she got distracted by her work. My sister never moved back home after she started at Harvard—escaping Ma's early morning vacuuming and shouting about how no one ever helped her—but when she came home for the holidays, it was game on. I was small enough to lean against the edge of the bathtub when she stuck an unsuspecting hand behind the shower curtain to flip the lever on. I'd listen to the shuffle of her wrestling her wool knit socks off and peeling off her hoodie and leggings. Just as she was sticking a lean, naked leg into the tub, her eyes would meet mine and she'd scream bloody murder.

"Katrina! You bitch!"

Ma was less amused when Maria was chasing me with a towel precariously wrapped around her body, water dripping off her leg, leaving puddles on the floor, a hairbrush for a weapon in her hand and revenge burning in her deep brown eyes.

Personally, I thought it was hilarious, but Maria wasn't my favorite victim.

Olivia was.

Livy was the middle child, and the perfect Scream Queen in the making. Not only was she a budding actress with her sights on Holly-wood, but she made scaring her downright too easy.

Keeping my footsteps featherlight and sneaking up on her in the kitchen while she was making herself a sandwich, she'd let out an eardrum-shattering screech.

Hiding behind her bedroom door… cue the blood-curdling shriek that earned me Ma's holler in Portuguese, *"Katrina Fatinha! Stop!"* from somewhere in the house.

I lived for the thrill of fucking with people, of scaring my family, of being scared myself.

Which was why I couldn't understand for the life of me what was so off-putting about these wax figures. Maybe it was the way their eyes seemed to follow us as we traversed around the room. The lifelessness in their human features. The nuances and detail that made them feel like they'd lunge for me.

I lurched back when it did just that, its arm distending out for me, a gruff "boo" falling from its lips. Adam caught me when I hit his chest, the roar of his laugh vibrating through me.

I frowned at the scare actor as he slunk back into place, returning to his sentinel state, awaiting his next unsuspecting victim.

"He got you good," Adam said, righting me back into place, his commanding hands lingering on my waist.

I blew out a raspberry, nodding my head weakly. Yeah, he and the other two actors who'd done the same thing in the last fifteen minutes when I'd gotten a little too close, trying to get a better look. Pulling out of Adam's hold, I hugged my upper body, running my fingers along the pimpled flesh on my arms. I'd knotted my coat around my waist, the heat from the mounting anxiety and adrenaline rush making me too warm.

I couldn't believe that this building wasn't a Halloween attraction three-hundred-and-sixty-five days of the year. They had transformed the galleries into a series of mazes, but beyond the disguises, the historicalness of the building's architecture and interior work was impossible to ignore—flying buttresses lined the arched stone ceiling, crown molding along the panels of the walls adorned by macabre paintings depicting hell and medieval executions, complimented by heavy drapery over stunning tracery on windows.

It was a labyrinth of eeriness. While the scare actors were a six-week addition, the phobia-inducing trepidation the stationary wax figures created all on their own was no joke.

A shriek up ahead startled me, ejecting me from my thoughts.

I watched as an actor charged toward a group of teenage girls up ahead, catching them off guard. They squealed, their circle splitting up. One shoved the other forward as a pleading sacrificial lamb, before bursting out into peals of laughter when she nearly toppled over from fright alone, her arms flailing miserably to keep herself upright.

Shaking my head, I released the embrace on myself, and exhaled the breath I'd been holding with control. Despite the beauty within the architecture, there was something not quite right about this place… and it wasn't just because of the theme of the event.

It was the figures themselves. I could chalk it up to paranoia, but there was something I just couldn't put my finger on about them that left me uneasy and my chest hitching with anxious breaths that failed to inflate my lungs.

After we'd crossed the threshold of the entrance, we worked our way through the first section of the museum, finding ourselves in a gallery paying homage to infamous American criminals and serial killers. There were tiny placards pitched nearby, identifying them, alongside a brief history lesson printed on paper in a hard plastic shell, illuminated by display lighting.

Try as I did to focus on the words, letting their story marinate in my mind, my focus would always wander back to their faces. The penetrating effect in their unblinking beady stare forced each hair on my body upright, an uncomfortable tingling stretching across my scalp.

It was disturbing how lifelike they were.

The extent of the details hand carved into their faces, their carefully selected clothes fitting their time period, meticulously pressed, not a wrinkle or crease to be found. Each strand of hair styled with care, lowlights catching on the dim lighting in the room.

But it was their immobility and the way their eyes created the illusion of stalking you around the room that sent my heart rate soaring, each beat pounding closer to a tachycardia.

The anticipation of what-if curdled the blood in my veins, my stomach roiling. I couldn't look away, no matter how much I wanted to. As though I was waiting for something to happen, and I needed to remain on guard until it did.

It was almost like beneath the wax… there were real people involuntarily trapped within their fiberglass frames, desperate to break out. Their eyes fixed. Limbs motionless and encased in wax. Eyelids glued in place. Their silent screams tunneling against the seal of their lips, trapped within their own mind.

I swallowed. Or maybe that was just my overactive imagination.

No one would go to that extent, and I'd spent too many nights on a Wikipedia rabbit hole, reading about some of the infamous murderers in the room with us. The lengths in which they'd gone to for the dopamine hit from the kill.

I eyed each figure with distrust as we wandered through the rooms. None of it was real. It was a form of art, someone's livelihood, but there was just something not right about this place.

"Check this one out," Adam called, canting his head toward Ed Gein—the Butcher of Plainfield—the inspiration of Leatherface from the *Texas Chainsaw Massacre* franchise.

Although, to my knowledge, there had been no actual chainsaws involved in his butchering.

Stubble lined his set jaw, his cheeks slightly hollowed in, his lips fixed in the faintest sneer like he didn't have a single fuck to give for any of his atrocities. Proud, glacial blue eyes stared right back at me, the left eye drooping just a little. His hair thinned at his hairline, the tufts unkept at the top and shorn near his protruding ears. Somehow, the inspiration of the movie was more terrifying than the Hollywood interpretation.

"I'm good right here."

"Baby," Adam began, trying to suppress the laugh and failing. "C'mere." He crooked a finger at me, and I narrowed my eyes at him with mistrust. "I promise I won't let anything get you…" he trailed off, licking his lips and dragging his teeth against his bottom lip, my stomach flipping at the suggestive gesture. "Nothing but me."

My body warmed, and my lips parted from the promise in those three words. That was one way to take the edge off. Adam extended an open palm out to me, and with a steadying intake, I found my nerve, and accepted his hand. His fingers clasped mine, and he lured me in gently, the hand that held mine letting me go, to twine his arm around my waist. He dropped his forehead against my temple, his free hand brushing my hair over my shoulder.

"You're prettiest when you're afraid."

I lifted my heavy eyes to his. "Oh, yeah?"

"Mhm," he hummed, grinding against me. "I don't love that someone else is scaring you, but…" his lips found the shell of my ear, "I'm willing to bet you're wet right now, huh?"

The blush stretched from the curve of my breasts, right up the length of my neck, and settled on my cheeks. My pussy pulsated in response to his confident observation, and small frissons of heat gathered under my belly button.

How well my husband knew me.

"Should I check?" he pondered, his voice low and raspy. He splayed his commanding fingers on my stomach, pressing down on me, driving me harder against him as he rolled his brazen hips. "Or should we keep going and see just how wet you can get?"

I swallowed, meeting the next gentle roll of his cock against my ass. "Keep going," I replied, panting.

He'd taught me that lust, adrenaline, and fear, all came from the same place. The momentum was only just beginning. He always kept me on the edge of the unknown, because it made the explosion of all my nerve endings giving into the euphoria so much better.

"Let's go, then." The groan resounded in the back of his throat as he extricated himself from me, like it physically pained him to create any kind of distance between us. I followed him through the throngs of people into an arched opening leading into the next section of the museum fixed in the middle.

My pulse punched in my throat as soon as we crossed the threshold, the ominous energy sucker punching me, earning the flaring of my eyes. The rest of the museum felt like Disneyland compared to this room and I would have gladly walked back out if my rabid curiosity didn't demand otherwise of me.

It was poorly lit in here, only it didn't seem intentional—no, it was like a deterrent. People fluttered in and out with disinterest... but not us. The further we walked, the worse the sick feeling twisting inside me grew, sweat beading along the back of my neck.

My mind screamed to leave, my strides slowing as though anvils had affixed to my feet, but I couldn't stop myself.

Small wall sconces flickered with dim orange bulbs, the temperature in here a few degrees colder than the rest of the building. We came to a standstill, taking in the room.

The discomfort forced every hair on my body upright, making it impossible to appreciate the room. Unlike the rest of the transformed chambers, this one seemed like it always looked this way. Tilting my head back, I followed the contour of the gilded ceiling, a grotesque Baroque-style painting above us. Where angels and heaven would have looked down on me had this been a church, there was nothing but a flamed landscape and gruesome winged beasts hugging the curve of the ceiling.

Hell.

I followed the sinister strokes of paint to the center, where the flames dispersed, and a Puritan woman shrouded by ivy existed, a juxtaposition to the destruction of the fire. Her pale skin contrasted the smoke and flames, her dress a brilliant red color and her copper hair set in tight curls with her hands clasped tight around something I couldn't make out. From what I could remember from school about the Puritans, they had a very strict code of colors they wore, and red was definitely not one of them.

There was also something strangely familiar about her, and I couldn't place it.

Who was that?

"The Rose of Rockchapel," Adam offered. I looked away from the ceiling, and found his head tipped toward the ceiling, his profile tense. "She was the daughter of one of those assholes." He jutted a finger to the center of the room, and I stared at the two fixed figures.

Wide-brimmed felt hats sat on top of shoulder-length hair—crisp, white ruffs stark against black doublets and breeches. Dark stockings held in place by garters, their frozen, sullen expressions staring beyond.

Before I could question who they were, Adam answered, "The Founding Fathers."

"The Founding Fathers," I echoed. I'd never heard of them before.

"They founded this town in the 1600s. Most of them fled Salem to escape the persecution of the Witch Trials."

My nose wrinkled. *Why?*

"Their viewpoints were unconventional. They didn't want to take the risk of the accusations flying around back then, so they bailed and set up shop here."

How had I never heard of this?

At my silence, he continued. "They're real people, but most of their history is built on urban legends," he said, scratching his jaw, the coarse stubble rasping under his calluses. "So much of what people said they did was fucked up…" he paused. "Even for me."

My eyebrows rocketed to my hairline. My husband wasn't a saint. That wasn't news to anyone in this town. He had a reputation that preceded him and secrets I would help him keep buried for as long as we both lived. So, for him to express discomfort by someone else's actions, I knew whatever had purportedly occurred must not have been good.

"What's her story?" I asked, unable to resist.

"She was Increase Walsh's daughter." He lowered his eyes from the ceiling, kicking his chin toward the shorter of the figures. "A magistrate." Adam folded his arms over his chest. "The story is that she loved a painter, and he loved her back. But they weren't allowed to be together because," he gestured toward the taller of the two figures, "she was supposed to marry Josiah Roberts' son."

I tracked Adam's unhurried strides toward the figures, his eyes narrowing. "Walsh's daughter and the painter tried to run away together, but they were caught at the border of Rhode Island." I could visualize it all so perfectly—two frantic silhouettes moving furtively through the depthless night, trusting only the stars above them to lead to them to their escape… only to have their love story cut short by people who were against them.

"They slit his throat right there in front of her," he said.

I lost my control of the gasp, my hand shooting to my mouth. Jesus Christ. Puritans means of upholding the law could be barbaric, but this was extreme for this kind of infraction. "For trying to run away?" I asked against the barricade of my fingers.

"Duty," he said simply. "You don't wrong a Founding Family, I guess. Even if their blood ran through you." He pivoted, stabbing the inside of his cheek with his tongue. "Their descendants still live in town." He looked unimpressed, sniffing. "When we were in high school, they said if you drove across the Runnins River bridge, toward the border, and flicked your headlights three times for every life they stole, you'd see her… or hear her."

My throat stretched around the gulp. Every life they stole? Wasn't it just the one?

He filled in the blank. "Rather than have their daughter embarrass them, they threw her off the clock tower in forced penance." He dropped his arms, hesitating. "She was pregnant."

Three lives stolen. Now it made sense.

I rocked back on my heels, the tension knotting in my shoulders as I stared out into the archway. People entered the gallery room and turned around when they realized what was in here.

"You okay?" Adam prompted.

I nodded soberly, meeting his eyes. Taking slow, deliberate steps over to him, I halted in front of the figures, staring up into their frozen faces. I hoped karma was as cruel to them as they'd been to her.

"There's one thing that's odd, though," Adam said.

"What's that?" I asked, looking his way.

"There's five Founding Fathers. There's three missing."

I glanced at the placard at their base, reading off the names.

He was right.

Five names, two figures.

Roberts.

Walsh.

Taylor.

Mather.

Alcock.

Where were the rest?

The chuckle he let out was dry and short. "I guess it doesn't matter," he said, reading my mind. "These assholes in ruffles all look the same. Most people can't tell them apart." He reached for my hand, ending the conversation. "Ready to get out of here?"

For some reason, I couldn't compel myself to leave. I opened my mouth to speak, but the chime of a grandfather clock going off in the corner of the room cut me off.

There was something almost allegorical about the gallery compared to its counterparts, as though there was a hidden meaning out in the open and no one could place it. Someone paid homage to the girl whose life their rules had stolen.

And now she looked down on them from above, while they remained in purgatory on earth below. The room felt like a warning.

I stared into the eyes of the one Adam had pointed out as her father, wondering how anyone who'd brought you into this world could do that to you without hesitation.

Had he suggested it?

Had his rank and place in his society been worth more than his own flesh and blood? His daughter's happiness?

"We won't be like that, right?" I asked softly, buying myself a little more time in here.

"Like what?"

"Shitty parents."

I'd been pregnant once when I was twenty. My ex bailed when he found out.

How could you be so stupid?

It had hurt at the time, being blamed for something I hadn't done on my own, but I realized quickly, I wasn't anywhere near ready to be someone's ma. Never mind raising my ex's child while I still felt like a kid myself.

My siblings were supportive of my decision. My ma, not so much. She wanted me to get married, have the kid.

But I couldn't. So, with Sean's help, I dealt with it. I didn't regret my decision, but every so often, when I heard a story like the Rose of Rockchapel's, my memories came back to me. The angry tears stung the back of my eyes, and my chest heaved a little. I felt the weight of chains digging into my wrists and the trepidation of feeling trapped again. I didn't regret my choice, it was the best one I made for myself at the time, but it altered the naïve way I viewed the world and the people my life had once orbited around.

People should be allowed to make their own choices about their own bodies. They should be allowed to love who they love and be who they were. They deserved families and parents who honored and respected those choices, too. Who didn't force them to make decisions that weren't theirs to make.

I never wanted to be like that.

Adam was more than aware of my abortion and how it had shaped me. He was as familiar with my trauma and my past as he was with the roadmap of my body.

"I just mean..." I swallowed, trying the sentence again. "I mean, we won't try to make them into someone they're not." Like my ma had tried to do with me. "We won't try to stop them from loving who they love."

A rumble vibrated in the back of his throat. "Within reason."

Huh? I glanced his way, watching as he layered his hands on top of his head, a terse sigh breezing through his slim nose. "If our kid brings home some little shit, I'm gonna break their fucking legs."

"Adam."

"No kid of mine is dating someone who doesn't deserve them," he argued, earning the eyes of a couple who turned around when they realized there wasn't much to see in the gallery room.

I tried to fight back the smile. "Ours," I corrected, pointing at myself with my thumb. "I'm the incubator." I fought the urge to smile at my joke. He was going to be an overprotective dad, and I pitied anyone who came knocking on our door. They wouldn't just have to contend with Adam.

They'd have to face Vince, Gabriel, and Maxwell, too.

The four of them would put them through the wringer just to prove their worth.

He smiled, but it was flimsy. "I'm serious, Trina." He lowered his arms, rolling out his stiff shoulders. I could hear the clicking of knots in his back. "I want the best for them and of them. And I don't mean I expect them to be a brain surgeon or something." His hazel eyes crinkled in the corner. "I want them to know that they can be anything and they can love who they love, but that person needs to reciprocate that, too. I don't want them accepting the bare minimum from anyone or offering someone their scraps, either." He blew out a breath. "I learned that the hard way. I don't want them repeating my mistakes."

That was impossible because they had us as their parents.

Our children wouldn't grow up to see a filtered-down version of love between their parents like I had. Of course, I'd known my parents loved each other, but it just wasn't always evident until my dad died. Ma's world stopped for her, and sometimes, I wasn't sure it ever really started turning for her again.

"They won't," I assured, leaning against him. No one was harder on himself than Adam. He still punished himself for the shit he'd put me through. There had been countless nights I'd spent tucked against him on the couch, our legs twined together, our attention on the television, but all the while, he tested the rings on my fingers, as though ensuring they were too tight to come off.

Like he was afraid.

Flexing on my toes, I grabbed a fistful of his hoodie at the chest, forcing him to bend and meet me halfway. His eyes lowered as I swept my lips against his, his exhale fanning against my face. He framed my face with his hands, his thumbs brushing against the arches of my cheekbones.

"We won't be shitty parents," he promised. "We won't be perfect. I mean, I've got the mouth of a fucking sailor and you're a mess on a good day."

"Hey!" I protested, twisting my fist in his hoodie, jerking him playfully. He grabbed my wrist, holding it tight against him, and snatched my lips with his, struggling to contain the smile.

Adam let me go, and my calves relaxed as I lowered my boots flat to the floor. "Can we get the hell outta here now?" he complained.

Nodding my head, I glanced back at the wax figures, giving them one last look. Now that I was this close, I realized they seemed newer than the other figures out in the gallery. Like they were more recent additions. The craftsmanship was different, and their wax had a sheen to it, like someone freshly poured it and it hadn't had enough time to set correctly. Flicking my eyes over their faces, I took in the details of their features—noses of different heights and widths, lines set near their mouths, tufts of hair curling at their necklines. Coming upon the one closest to me, my heart stuttered to a stop and dread pushed through my pores when its left eye strained with a half twitch as though it had attempted to blink.

What in the actual fuck?

Was I seeing things? I held my breath, willing the damn thing to do it again. Blue eyes bulged and shook, the red veins protruding before it relaxed once more.

"It blinked," I blurted, my knees wobbling.

Holy fucking shit. It. Blinked. At. *Me.*

Or attempted to, anyway.

"What?" Adam questioned from behind me.

I lifted a shaking hand to the shorter figure, pointing at it. "*He* blinked." He, because it was no longer just an inanimate object. What the hell was going on in here?

"Your eyes are playing tricks on you," Adam assured, shaking his head. His chuckle was tight. "They're not real."

Yeah, tell that to someone who hadn't believed in Santa Claus until she was fifteen. Gritting my teeth, my shoulders squared. I knew how it sounded, but... I knew what I saw, too.

"Adam, I'm telling you," I argued, staring into the face of the shortest of the Founding Father figures. That son of a bitch had stared directly at me and attempted to communicate with me somehow. Glancing around the room, I studied the corners, finding the flicker of the security camera in the corner.

Was someone else watching us right now?

Confident in a way I hadn't been all night, I engaged in a staring contest with the damn thing, imploring those waxy lids to twitch. I willed its eyes to shift again, but they didn't.

But I knew what I saw.

My eyes stung, the dry air getting the better of me until I couldn't stand it anymore and blinked rapidly to compensate.

Gritting my teeth, I met my husband's dubious stare, my heart sinking. He didn't believe me.

Adam rubbed his forehead, exhaling. "Baby," he began, leaning over and touching the figure's hand. "As much as I hate him, Wagner's good at what he does. So were his grandfather and dad. It's a known thing throughout town that their figures have a tendency to make you believe they're real."

But I ignored him. I concentrated on the figures, waiting for something. The roving of eyes, a blink, the distension.

Anything at all to fortify my claim.

Adam's knuckles knocked against the figure's hand, a hollowed sound greeting us to demonstrate its lifelessness. "This place will mess with your head if you allow it to. He designed it that way."

My features collapsed into a frown, my pounding pulse drumming in my ears as I glanced back at the immobile figure again.

I knew what I saw, didn't I?

Raking my fingers through my orange hair, frustration took over the anxiety. My logic and emotions were at war with one another. What was I really insinuating here? That there were people inside of the figures? Adam had already showed me by touching them. Not a scare actor. Not a person.

Just wax. Inanimate. Frozen.

So maybe he was right. Maybe this place was just playing tricks on me. It had been a long day, and I'd been up since five.

Blowing up into my bangs, I offered him a quick nod, conceding. "Okay." But it didn't stop me from peering at the figure one final time, waiting for a sign that would never come.

CHAPTER FIVE

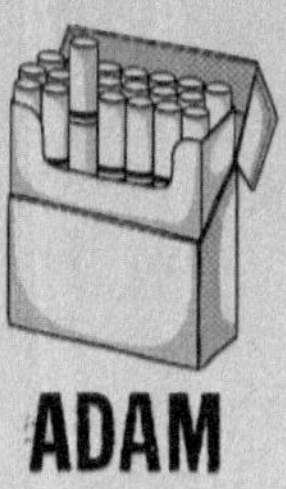

My phone vibrated in the pocket of my jogger as we stepped back out into the smoky main gallery, people milling around us in the fog, blue light pushing through while the bass of the music vibrated through the floors and thrummed loudly. My fingers brushed against my smokes before snagging on my phone.

I raised a brow, reading the message preview from Vince.

I'm heading out. You kids have fun.

Katrina leaned against me, flexing on her toes and craning her head to see. She was so nosy. Always had been, always would be. Shit, that nosiness had cost us our relationship. Indulging her, I lowered the phone and angled it her way so she could read it. She let out an ornery snort, glancing up at me through her false lashes. "Why the fuck did he even come if he was just going to bail?"

'Cause it was Vince. Why did he do half the shit he did? Nothing he ever did made sense to anyone. Shrugging, I put my phone back in my pocket, slinging an arm around her shoulders. She didn't sink against me like she normally did when she was content, a dead tip-off.

"What's wrong?"

"Nothing," she offered flatly, keeping her profile trained straight ahead.

Bullshit. I'd know if something was wrong from a state away. Everything about her changed right down to the notes of her rose garden perfume which I swore had the range of a mood ring and shifted from sweet and floral to sharp and menthol.

I narrowed my eyes, hunting for the truth, but she ignored me.

A scare actor came barreling toward us, deciding her obliviousness made her the perfect target.

His unrestrained cackle was like a foghorn over the music. Half of his face was missing. Prosthetics created the illusion of a dislocated jaw, the gruesome bone protruding, showing off the gory interior with flesh hanging from the skin. The other half of his face shrouded with pustulous boils formed in tight circles. The visual was more uncomfortable than the other half of his face, forcing the hair along my arms to stand upright. I had the stomach for a lot of things the average person didn't. But something about clustered dots admittedly made me a bit squeamish in a way nothing else did.

"Why don't you smile, pretty girl?" he demanded, releasing another shrill cackle.

She offered him nothing in return.

He attempted another angle, holding a blade up at his side, the tip glistening with fake blood. Unnaturally vomit-green eyes bore down on her, engaging her in a staring contest I knew he wouldn't win. His slash of lips twisted with a wide, toothy smile, the whites glowing under the blue light.

She folded her arms over chest, staring up at him like he was wasting her time. "Why don't you fucking make me?" she dared, her eyes turning into whetted daggers tipped with poison. "I'm so sick and tired of men telling women to smile."

The actor dropped the act, holding his hands upright in defense, his grip on the knife loosening. "Just doin' my job, lady," he said, a New England accent replacing the contrived voice he'd been using.

I'd bet "Down with the Patriarchy for $800" wasn't on his Jeopardy board tonight.

He shot off in another direction, procuring the screams he'd been looking for from another couple.

Yeah, there was nothing wrong alright. "Katrina."

She ground her molars, the column of her neck tensing as she raised her stubborn chin. "I know what I saw, okay?" she challenged, still refusing to meet my stare.

I groaned. Christ, not this.

Her pert nose wrinkled, her septum piercing wiggling. "And I know that sounds ridiculous, but…" Her lips pursed with displeasure, followed by the framing of her forehead with her hand. "He blinked at me, Adam." She dropped her hand against her thigh, her weight shifting from foot to foot as she trapped the fabric of her dress in her fingers until her knuckles whitened. "Or tried to, anyway. I have no reason to make that up."

My jaw tightened. Did I think my wife was hallucinating?

Short of seeing it for myself, I couldn't confirm jack shit. So here was what I knew for certain. This place didn't have oddities in its name for no reason.

Things were peculiar in here. They always had been.

It had an aura to it that would follow you home if you allowed it to and a history that kept you up at night if you believed in it.

People who came in but never came back out.

Police reports that led nowhere.

Moulage faces adorning walls that seemed so familiar.

Hidden stairwells serving as another network within the edifice.

Cautionary allegories painted on ceilings.

Whatever Vince was up to, I sensed it had something to do with this place.

Which meant I was going to get roped into this at some point because we were a family and that's what family did—cleaned up each other's messes, and made some together, too.

Blowing out a terse breath, I said, "I believe you."

She straightened, her chin lifting to disguise her shock. "Really?"

"Yeah." I sniffed, the motes of dust in the air messing with my sinuses. Looking down at Katrina over my nose, I met her hopeful eyes. "I believe you're overtired and horny and your imagination is getting the best of you."

I'd always loved her scared for that reason. She was more impressionable and pliant. Her fear acted as her playbook. The harder her heart walloped, the faster my blood pressure surged. I was entranced by the enthralling, rhythmic beats of the organ keeping her alive. Hungry for a taste.

Her anger on the other hand… it turned those soft honey-brown orbs into dark pools that promised violence. Her lush lips pushed into a sneer as she raked her hair aggressively behind her ears. "You're an asshole, Adam," she snapped.

"But I'm your asshole," I reminded, inclining my head, smirking down at her. "Doesn't that count for something?"

She shook her head, storming from my side, the muscles in her back knitting together. "Shoulda stayed in Fall River," she mumbled under her breath, creating more distance between us.

It didn't matter how loud the music was in this place, or how many voices competed over hers, when she was nearby, my hearing became ultrasonic.

My futile attempts at levity fled the premises. She did not just fucking say that.

To even *think* that… it forced unbidden memories to resurface.

I snatched her wrist, her shoulder straining under the movement. I hauled her into me, a small puff of air leaving her lips at the unexpected motion as she collided against my hard body.

"Let go."

"Never," I hissed, the conversation too reminiscent of the one we'd had last November when I'd found her on a date with some clown who hadn't deserved to even share the same oxygen as her.

I meant it then as much as I meant it now.

She stilled for a beat of a moment, but less than ten seconds later, she was fighting against me. But it was pointless. She was ensnared. Mine. Trapped.

Nothing more than a little rabbit who found herself cornered in a wolf's den.

I wasn't letting her go for shit.

The humor was absent from her eyes, her chest rising and falling rapidly with each tense breath she took.

"What did you say under your breath, Little Rabbit?" I demanded, engaging in a standoff with her.

All she did was glower, attempting to burn a hole straight through my cranium. Her lips tugged a little to the right, pouting.

The prolonged silence threatened to choke us both, but neither one of us was going to give in to the other.

But I needed her to.

My heart drummed against my chest, threatening to punch right through the inked-cracked cavern in the center of my chest in offering to her. I'd had the chest piece tattooed a little after my ma passed, a few months after Katrina and I had broken up years ago.

It was to serve as a reminder to myself to remain heartless because people could hurt you if you let your guard down. The problem was, after years of being apart, once Katrina was physically back on my radar, I was consumed by her and unwilling to give her up to anyone —my brothers included.

The depths of my hatred and betrayal could never change that. They'd wielded that to their advantage.

She mended the abyss and undid everything I thought I knew about myself. She challenged me and became the life source of my strength, my beacon in a dark place.

Which was why she didn't get to say shit like that to me. I didn't care how pissed she was.

I didn't give two shits if she hadn't meant it or said it out of frustration. Anything that sounded close to her fantasizing about a life without me in it—without her here within reach of me—wasn't something I'd ever allow her to entertain, in her head or out loud.

She could call me anything she wanted. An asshole, a sociopath.

She could threaten to expose me, and I'd fuck the idea right out of her. I'd tattoo my name on her body just as I'd done hers on mine so she could never forget who she belonged to.

But she couldn't leave me.

She wasn't allowed to even insinuate it.

"Nothing," Katrina faltered, paling a little.

"No," I urged, grit lining my throat. "Say. *It.*"

"You *heard* me," she accused, already sounding contrite despite her frown. "Why bother repeating myself?"

"'Cause I want you to look me in the eye," I charged, my voice growing raspy, my stare boring into hers. "And tell me you'd rather be anywhere else but with me."

I wanted to hear her say that her life was so much better without me in it so I could call bullshit.

I loomed over her, forcing her spine to straighten. Pink stained her cheeks, but she refused to cow to me. Just how I liked her. Defiant. *Mine.*

"Adam, there are people watching."

"I don't give a fuck." Let them watch. Let them see how much I loved this pipsqueak that I'd sooner burn this whole place to the fucking ground with these people trapped inside than entertain any kind of thought where she wasn't my fucking everything. I'd kneel on glass for her, bleed all over the place to prove it, rip my heart out and hand it to her still beating if it made her smile.

If she hadn't wanted that, too, she should have stayed the fuck out of Elara Park.

"I was kidding," she offered, her resolve weakening. When I didn't reply, she wiggled her mouth from side to side, watching me from under her long false lashes. The band was lifting in the corner. "Okay?"

No. Not okay. I didn't like her hypotheticals where our relationship was called into question. She could come at me about anything else and I'd take it on the chin, but when it came to her or us—it was a no-fly zone.

"No. Not okay." My free hand bolted around her jaw, tipping her chin upward, her puffy lips parting. The base of my fist leaned against her urgent pulse, its beats resonating through my whole body like it was my own life force. Like my survival entirely depended on hers. The truth of the matter was, it did. I hadn't been living up until I found her again. I was existing. Balancing on the precipice of life and death because I didn't see the fucking point anymore.

She had given me a reason to breathe again, to wake up. "I don't like your jokes. I like mine better."

"Oh?" I released both her jaw and wrist, but before she got comfortable being out of my reach, I spooled an arm around her slender waist, forcing her feet on top of mine just like we always did at home.

Our home.

Where her things existed. Where we built our life together. Paid bills and made meals and argued over stupid shit like her collection of empty shampoo bottles on the shower ledge that always fell over when I got into the shower or the fact that I ate her string cheese. I didn't even like string cheese, but I liked getting her riled up. I loved her in our parlor where she wove Saoirse's hair into thick French braids every night while my kid sister sat on the floor between my wife's legs and they watched an episode of *True Blood* together and I hollered at Katrina to close her mouth every time Eric Northman was on the screen.

Not that I blamed her entirely. I'd probably simp for that pale, muscular fuck if dicks did it for me.

She always offered me a flirty little smile in response, reminding me with her eyes alone that even if he appeared right in front of her, she'd still choose me. 'Cause he wasn't the one who made her a custom kitchen table with a pile of wood sourced from an old house she'd worked on restoring. Wood no one saw any beauty in but her. He wasn't the one who sat in a closet with her during a panic attack and opened his arms to her when she was ready. And it sure as shit wasn't his calves dealing with the frigidness of her frozen feet every night.

It was me.

She belonged with me. In our bed, at our table, in our home.

Not back in Fall River, closer to her family, far away from me and the life we were building together. Our empire. Our fucking legacy.

We were raising our kids in Rockchapel. They were going to the same schools I'd gone to. They were going to drive across the Runnins River bridge, flash their lights three times and tell some bullshit story at school the next day about how they'd seen the Rose of Rockchapel. Then I was going to ground the fuck out of them for burning the gas in our car over something so stupid.

"You wanna be an adrenaline junky? I'll show you."

She didn't get to run back to her hometown or imply she would when she got upset with me. I'd hunt her down and drag her back kicking and screaming.

"I don't like it when you deny my reality," she said, her palms flattening against my chest. She worried her bottom lip with her teeth. "It just…" she blew an exhale up into her bangs, her warm breath wafting over my face. "It makes me feel like shit… like I'm…" she didn't complete her sentence.

She didn't have to.

That was the last thing I wanted.

"I'm not trying to make you feel like shit," I began, looping her hair behind her ear. "Or deny your reality." Whatever the hell that meant. "I'm trying to get you to focus."

Focus on what mattered. Not on Rhys Wagner's creepy fucking form of art. On me, on us, on spending our first night out together in months. We spent so much time at home or out with my brothers that we missed out on actual date nights where I got to show her off to the rest of the world.

I didn't want her spending tonight inside her head, worrying about shit she didn't need to worry about.

None of it was real, and if I said it enough times, I might believe it, too.

She shook her head, undoing the lock of her hair. Her expression pinched again, her feathery brows bending in the middle. "It tried to blink at me, Adam. I know it did."

"Say it did, then what?" I asked, indulging her.

She tucked her chin into her neck, avoiding my stare. She hadn't thought that far ahead. My tattooed knuckles ran under her jaw, returning her stare to mine. Her soft sigh wafted across my hand. "I don't know."

"There are a bunch of explanations. Maybe Rhys is testing out an animatronic feature." Even that sounded wrong.

No one made that kind of investment on figures here. In Boston, where the ticket sales would have justified the investment from the foot traffic and publicity alone? Sure.

In *Rot*chapel… no.

But what was the alternative? He was hiding living people inside of wax figures?

An icy chill worse than Katrina's feet in January crept up my spine.

That sounded too fucked, even for me.

But the whispering of my primitive instincts assured me it wasn't outlandish and that maybe, just maybe, she had a reason to be on edge in that room.

My molars met, crushing together until pain smarted up my temple and pounded behind my eyes. What better way to hide a string of bodies than right out in the open? I'd be impressed if the concept wasn't so fucking cocky and on-brand of him.

"Maybe," she agreed weakly, defeated. "I'm sorry I said that."

Clearing my throat, I pushed the thought away. "I'm sorry I gave you a reason to." Sure, I enjoyed getting her all fired up, but I didn't like hurting her or giving her any motivation to think that I didn't believe in her or respect her opinions.

Or delusions.

Any residual anger melted away. I'd taken a page out of her brother's unsolicited marital advice after we'd told them we'd eloped. After the initial shock and Sean's "welcome to the family spiel", he'd hauled me outside, out of earshot of everyone else, to read me the riot act for our impulsivity.

When it became clear to him this wasn't a hasty attempt at entrapping his kid sister after losing her for a second time, but intentional and well thought out—at least on my side—he changed his tune. *"Let me offer you some advice, Adam. Arguments are inevitable in any relationship, especially a marriage. Remember to repair as soon as you're both receptive."*

I had always held a lot of respect for her brother, but that was probably the soundest advice he'd ever offered me and I'd taken it to heart.

We didn't make a habit of staying in conflict for very long. We'd spent too many years apart to invest more than a few minutes upset with each other. Arguing was inevitable. She was a stubborn pain in the ass and my default mode of operation was flipped on to "asshole" even on a good day. I didn't want her to temper who she was, any more than I believed she wanted me to be as pious as Christ himself.

That wasn't who we were. It wasn't what drew us to each other.

Her pronounced teeth flashed, finding her bottom lip. "You were right."

"About?"

Her soft tits pressed against my rib cage, her fiery eyes flashing up to mine. "I am overtired and horny. This place is giving me an adrenaline rush and I wanna finish what we started in the car."

Now *that*, that I could get behind. And I had the perfect place in mind. "Oh, yeah?"

She nodded. My hands slid to her tiny hips, the bone brushing against my palms. Guiding her off my feet, I directed her deeper through the crowd, beelining back toward the darkened gallery room with the Founding Fathers in it. I detected her footfalls slowing when she sensed where we were going.

"Adam…"

I knew she didn't like it in there even if she had been curious about the room, but she had to trust me. The first step to exposure therapy was recognizing that the only way out was through. Sitting in the discomfort was inevitable. What better way to get over your newfound phobia than by fucking your way out of it?

Giving her perspiring hand a comforting squeeze, she returned my grip in stride, finding her nerve. Regardless of what she thought she'd witnessed—and what I was beginning to question myself—this room was perfect for what I had in store for her.

I'd known it as soon as I'd spotted the niche in the wall. It was as though the alcove had been designed for debauched people just like us who wanted to fuck within sight for anyone curious enough to come closer.

Spotting the recess in the wall, I guided her toward it. "Where are we going?" Katrina asked with a nervous laugh, her fear beginning to become an afterthought. I ushered her into the cavity, thrusting her spine against the wall, bracketing my hand against the back of her head to protect her.

The thrill had my blood pumping through my veins, a gnawing hunger chewing through my stomach and heat building in my balls.

I tapped the inside of her boots, forcing her legs apart so I could step between them, her dress straining.

"Where do you belong?" I asked her, bringing my face close to hers.

Her long neck worked with a swallow, her eyes growing heavy. "With you."

"And where's that?"

She drew in a shuddering breath. "In Rockchapel."

Bracing one forearm above her head, I leaned into her and squeezed her hip with my other hand, a pulse forming under my fingers. "Where in Rockchapel?"

"At home."

I nodded. "Whose house is that?"

"You—" I interrupted the thought, my fingers digging into her bony hip, the sharp yelp falling from her lips had my cock straining. "*Our* home," she corrected.

"That's right, Little Rabbit. You belong here in Rockchapel with me, in our home, because you're mine. You understand that, don't you?"

Mine.

She was in an absolute daze, her chest working overtime to catch up with her labored breaths, her pupils dilating.

"Nod your head." Katrina forced her eyes to widen, her head weaving. "And I'm yours." The hand clutching her hip descended, my fingers brushing against the outside of her thigh, sending her flexing on her toes. Her head lulled to the right, bending her neck in an offering to me. I sloped forward, feathering my lips softly against her hammering, heady pulse. Each pump felt closer to a stroke against my cock. I tested the cord in her neck with my teeth, her breathy intake musical in my ears.

Footsteps registered in my ears as people neared the Founding

Father figures. "Who's this asshole?" a guy with a thick New England accent announced, breaking out into a laugh.

"One of the Founding Fathers, I think," a nasally female voice replied.

"Looks like a douche."

Katrina's eyes flared as I gathered the fabric of her dress upward, my hand slipping under it. I gripped her upper thigh and her head fell back, her lips parting and her eyes lowering.

"Adam," she murmured as my fingers inched closer to the heated juncture where her thigh met the apex of her pussy, saliva pooling in my mouth at the thought. Her legs parted as wide as the dress would allow her to, and I sunk to my knees.

Now I was gonna taste her.

"Ugly son of a bitch," the man announced, his voice closer now. "Look at him."

"He's kinda cute," the woman said.

My wife's fingers sunk into my hair, her nails scraping against my scalp. I bunched her dress at her waist. Resting my forehead against her taut stomach, I caught the muted glint of her belly button ring. My teeth snagged the bow on her panties, grinding against the flimsy thread, affixing it in place, teasing her. Her arousal permeated, the throes of excitement warming my chin. Her grip on my hair tightened as I dragged my teeth downward, coming upon her clit.

"Ah," she hissed out upon contact.

I laughed against her, rolling my eyes upward to meet hers. "They might hear you."

"Good," she replied. "Maybe they'll see all the dirty things you do to me when you think no one's watching."

My fingers toyed along the tiny seashell stitching against the leg band of her panties. "My favorite thought is someone seeing how fucking pretty you look with my cock inside of you."

Tunneled inside her mouth with saliva dribbling over her chin and tears leaking from her eyes with my fingers wrenched in her hair to keep her in place.

In her tight little cunt where I kept my punishing strokes short and firm, driving myself into her with a brutality she felt under her belly button that only she'd ever been able to handle.

Burrowed inside the stretched ruffled ring between her full plump ass cheeks, I'd worked in over the months since I'd gotten her back. I liked her on all fours while I sank into her inch by delicious inch, while one of her hands gripped helplessly at whatever was under her to keep her in place while she played with herself with the other.

She was the most beautiful fucking thing I'd ever seen, and I wanted everyone to know it. I wanted them to know who made her come, whose cum she swallowed, whose name she cried out.

Me.

The guy all of five feet away from us let out a throaty laugh to his female companion. "I expect nothin' less from someone who doles out pity fucks to half the town."

Katrina lifted an eyebrow, unimpressed.

"Jackass," the woman spit out, storming off.

"Aw, c'mon, Sarah. I'm just playin'. Come back." He chased after her.

We lost our audience. "I want them to come back," I taunted, running my mouth along the fleshy inside of her thigh, her breath shuddering. "I want someone to watch me feast on you."

She lifted her eyes, guiding my attention to the camera above us, the red light flickering, indicating it was recording. "Someone already is," she guaranteed.

I lowered my eyes, glancing in the direction of the sentinel Founding Fathers, staring directly back at us. "Then let's give 'em a show worth watching, Little Rabbit."

CHAPTER SIX

KATRINA

WITH MY RIGHT THIGH SLUNG OVER HIS SHOULDER, ADAM TUGGED MY panties to the side, tucking them over my swollen labia, the cold draft in the air lingering over the heat of my skin. He ran his tongue along his bottom lip, his eyes darkening as though he were already feasting on me.

My leaking pussy fluttered in response, my inner muscles contracting and squeezing around nothing, accompanied by the phantom sensation of him stretching me just by the way he studied me from below.

I loved being his favorite fixation.

His lifelong obsession.

His wife.

He inclined his body forward, and I tracked his hand as he closed it around the stiff tenting in his joggers, the anticipation registering under my spine.

"Look at you," he said hoarsely, his teeth digging against his bottom lip. "So fucking pretty and ready for me, huh?" His knuckles whitened when he clenched at himself, his thumb seating itself against my entrance, circling me in delirium-inducing circles. My thighs quivered, fighting to keep me upright, the tiny mewl slipping free from my lips.

A lock of his mahogany hair slipped across his forehead, his head slanting, his expression fixed with concentration while he teased my slit, gathering my cream along the pad of his finger and dragging it upward. My equilibrium almost tilted on its axis and my hands brandished to his shoulders to keep me upright when he brushed against my clit, a million nerve endings in my body singing with life. Adam's dark and throaty chuckle reverberated through me, something promissory in the vibration.

The short edges of my fingernails fisted the fabric of his hoodie when his lips closed around my clit, his teeth brandishing the nub for a beat of a second before replacing them by the deep, intoxicating pulls between his lips. I threw my head back, my hair gliding along the wall while the muscles in my left thigh cramped and screamed at me.

I wouldn't stop this for anything. The pain was delicious.

The suction on his mouth lessened, his tongue flattening against my clit, circling around me. Adam's arresting hazel eyes rolled up to me, browner than they were green in this moment. The shadows from the muted light in the distance played against his sharp features. I had the weighted feeling that despite the room being absent of people; we weren't alone.

My skin prickled, every hair on my body upright, detecting a threat despite there being none. But that wasn't entirely true, was it? Within these four walls, someone—something—was always watching.

There was a term for this.

Scopaesthesia. The paranoia provoking phenomenon of being watched without identifying the source.

But we had a source, didn't we?

I lifted my head, staring at the wax figure, who stared right back, frozen. I'd known what I'd seen, heard its silent struggle and unspoken plea behind its sealed lips.

They'd been watching us just as much as we'd been watching them.

There couldn't be people behind those layers of wax, no matter how hard my mind wanted to convince me otherwise. It was an illusion, an atmospheric farce, much like the rest of this place. Where the structure communed with you and inanimate objects tracked you in lifeless interest while your gaze-detection radar went nuclear.

A chill followed the thought, crawling up my spine like a sickening traipse of fingers. I stared up at the flicker of the closed-circuit camera, the slow blink of the red light hypnotizing me, my pulse storming wildly in my throat. But its lure was no match against the brandishing of Adam's deft tongue, swirling along my core, followed by the sensory shift of his playful nips, coaxing me back to him.

This place couldn't contend with the magnitude of him. No matter how hard it tried.

It wasn't real.

Adam was. My husband was the only one who could haunt me, love me, and fuck with me.

I ran my fingers against the mahogany-and-chocolate stubble on his cheek when he leaned back on his haunches to appraise me, his cheek sinking into my palm, reveling in my touch with lidded eyes. It gave me a chance to catch my breath, to savor the man—the predator—who kneeled at my feet, his arm working furiously against his sheathed shaft while he worshipped me like I was the only thing in the world that mattered to him. It had been he who'd taught me that through fear, we could find ourselves. Through adrenaline, we were limitless.

When Adam had enough of my reverence, his eyes molted, and he was back to business again. He sucked each labium, releasing them with an audible pop, the folds glistening in a combination of my body's eager responses and his saliva. He ran his tongue from my clit down to my pulsating opening, that unrelenting muscle driving home deep inside me.

All the air fled my lungs, my sharp cry freeing ceiling-ward, twisting with the chorus of Type O Negative's "Black No.1." My hands shot for his hair, grasping tight at the roots, and twisting with a desperation to keep him fixed there. The command of my grip earned me his throaty groan, the sound throbbing against my pussy. His audible feasting of me sent another frisson of need rocketing through me, my climax within my reach as I concentrated on the chase of that ephemeral plunge of ecstasy.

I flexed on my toes, grinding urgently against his starved mouth, and he made a deep growl of approval, pleasure gathering under my spine.

"That's it, Little Rabbit," he rasped out between the rocking of my hips, opening his mouth wider. "Take what only I can give you."

I ground myself back and forth, and he matched my rhythm, his taut, deft tongue dipping in and out of me, the tip of his nose pushing against my clit, cutting off his breathing. He didn't seem to care, either. He just held me closer, driving me to that precipice of pleasure I was so desperate to plunge myself from in a free-fall. My thighs closed around his face, his stubble chafing against my thighs as my nerve endings coiled with warning.

"Come on my face, baby," he urged, jerking himself faster, sweat beading along his hairline. "Let this whole fucking museum hear how well you scream for me." The leg hooked over his shoulder pinned him to me when the dam broke and the orgasm cascaded over me, sending pinpricks of white dots behind my lidded eyes. My head swelled, every wayward thought and doubt I had fled. I gushed around his mouth and he sucked my body's nectar in desperate tugs, not daring to miss a single drop.

He leaned back on his haunches to study me, his lips swollen and sleek, his fingers roving over my leaking slit lazily, gathering what lingered of my release on his long fingers. My chest heaved while I fought to regulate my breathing and I tracked his undulating frame as Adam rose to his feet, his expression slated with drunken heat. He licked his glossy lips and brought his fingers to my mouth, commanding me in silence. I bent forward, holding his stare, as I opened my mouth and accepted his offering. My cheeks hollowed around his fingers, tasting the familiar earthiness of my taste on his fingers, earning his flared nostrils when he drew his fingers back.

"My turn," he demanded. His hands closed around my shoulders, forcing me to my knees. He knew I went more than willingly. There was only one man I prayed to.

On my descent, my fingers hooked on the waistline of his joggers, tugging them over the curve of his muscular ass. His cock sprung out in greeting for me, and my right hand closed around his shaft, guiding him into the heated cavern of my mouth, the tang of his precum dancing on my palate.

The velvet of his shaft inside of my mouth betrayed the rest of him. He was rigid with deep, responsive veins, twitching with every bob of my eager mouth fraught to swallow him down in heady pulls.

My left hand slid under his shirt, relishing in the feel of his hard abdomen, reaping more of the pearled trickling of his release I greedily lapped up and swallowed.

"Fuck," he bit out as my lips enveloped him and I ran my tongue from the base to the tip, gliding my tongue around the crown of his cock. His inked fingers with my name tattooed across his knuckles sank into my hair, driving me down on him until I thought I'd choke. He thrusted against the back of my throat, my gag reflex coming online, tears stinging the back of my eyes. I felt his arresting stare on me, and I shifted mine to meet his, staring at him from behind my lashes.

Adam's mouth popped open, his eyes half-lidded as he kept me pinned in place and jerked his hips forward and back, finding a cadence with his hips, my tongue curving along his shaft. Every time he drew himself back, I used that as an opportunity to catch my breath and anticipate the next contact at the back of my throat.

"God, no one's ever sucked my cock as well as you have," he praised. "You were made for me, weren't you, Little Rabbit?"

I nodded as best as I could, the tears I'd tried to contain leaking from my eyes, no doubt smearing my eyeliner. I didn't care, though. My tears won me his grunt of satisfaction at the sight, his face twisting with pleasure. He released one hand from my hair, swiping the tear away with his thumb, bringing it to his mouth to sample. "Even your tears taste good." He exhaled, his eyes burning. Adam drew his hoodie upward, gathering it under his chest to create a better viewpoint, flashing me his defined abdomen. I loved the sight of my fingers splayed against the planes of muscle, the reflection of the red flicker from the camera above us catching on my wedding and engagement ring. The reminder that we were never alone.

Someone was always watching.

"Your lipstick looks so good painting my cock, baby," he commented, breathless. I moaned around him, and he grunted under the vibration. His stomach hardened under my regard as though he were preening for me as I worked him, leaving a smeared ring of dark lipstick along his veined shaft. The waxy bite of my lipstick was nothing compared to the heady and potent taste of him. My pussy fluttered at the visual, my coiled body desperate for the carnal driving of his body thrusting inside of mine.

Adam forced me upright, his self-control unraveling. My legs stumbled as he backed me up against the wall. Guiding his cock to my pussy, he spread my swollen folds, gliding himself back and forth, collecting my arousal on his shaft. He tapped my sensitive clit with the head of his cock, holding my eyes as he did, greedily taking in every shift of my breathing. My charged nerve endings were already igniting with the promise of another impending orgasm. Adam pinned an arm under my thigh, hoisting my leg upward roughly. Lining himself up at my entrance, he slammed himself against me until he bottomed out, driving my spine up the wall.

I couldn't contain the cry, its desperation echoing in the tiny cavity we were hiding in.

"Fuuuuuck, Katrina," he croaked against my throat. "You feel so fucking good." My hands slid to his ass again, my nails leaving little half-moons against the smooth flesh, trying to keep him as close to me as possible. "Pull down your dress. Let me see your pretty tits."

My hands slipped to the sweetheart neckline of the dress, peeling the dress down over the teardrop swells peppered in purple demarcations in varying shades from the abuse of his mouth over the last few days. My pierced nipples tightened to stiff points, the draft in the alcove swirling over my goose-pimpled skin. Adam adjusted my body's positioning against the wall, his tongue laving across the lotus inked on my sternum, his mouth gliding to the left and closing around my tit, vacuuming the tiny swell into his punishing mouth.

He toyed with the piercing with his tongue, introducing another sensory element with the addition of the straight, blunt edges of his teeth, nipping at my nipple. My charged cry filled my ears, and he shifted his treatment to the other tit just as shadows fell across the alcove accompanied by voices muted over the pounding of music, growing clearer as they moved.

My attention twisted in the sound's direction, the risk of being caught sending another surge of adrenaline and lust through me.

A couple of guys gathered around the Founding Fathers, making a lewd gesture in front of the figures for a selfie. All the while completely oblivious to the debauchery that was going on a little further down the hall.

"You like it just as much as I do, don't you?" Adam asked over my lips, the cold tip of his twice-pierced nose pressed against mine, his eyes flickering from them to me. "You love the thrill of people watching us?"

People.

The camera above us.

The wax figures.

I nodded.

I loved being his, and everyone knowing it.

No one could touch me but him.

Adam lowered me to the ground, drawing himself out, my need smearing against my thigh. I whimpered at the loss of him, and he twisted me around, guiding my splayed hands to the wall. He kicked my feet apart and angled my body to bend. His knuckles brushed against the plump contour of my ass, directing his cock back to its rightful home. His fingers closed around mine as he thrust inside me, my attention tipped toward the people.

They still hadn't realized.

Adam's tempo quickened, my body absorbing each brandishing, the slick squelch of my pussy practically turning my body boneless, my moans becoming more urgent.

We were going to get caught.

And I didn't care.

I didn't care because I was the freest with him—free of inhibition or the plagued rules of society. With him, I was an invincible wolf—his equal—not the scared, timid rabbit I'd always believed myself to be.

Adam's fingers hooked around my throat, squeezing my airways until my vision spotted and my heart drummed. I clenched around his cock as the second orgasm snuck up on me, and I shattered. Euphoria robbed me of all cognizant thought, and my head tipped back, the sharp cry wrenching free from my lips.

"What the hell was that?" one guy asked. From my peripheral, he leaned forward, but I didn't meet his eyes.

Adam wrenched my head to meet his hungry lips, devouring me as his strokes found their momentum again. His tongue dipped into my mouth, lashing against my own, his fingers clutching firmly against my jaw, claiming me.

"Oh shit," someone said, followed by a breathy chuckle. "I think…"

Their curiosity was Adam's kryptonite. His body practically swelled. His thrusts quickened, short and desperate, like he refused for there to be an inch of space between us.

"No fucking way," another voice blurted.

My husband made an urgent sound of desperation, and my body moved against him, beckoning his release. He gripped me fiercely, binding me in place, his lips eating up mine. Warmth flooded me, his cock kicking as he came inside of me, groaning out a "fuck" into my mouth.

He broke the kiss, satiated, as he examined my face. "Are you a rabbit or a wolf?" he murmured.

It was the same question every time. Some people got "I love you" post coitus—I got the reminder of just how far I'd come.

Wolves were fearless. They mated for life.

"A wolf where it counts," I replied, wetting my lips, rolling them together. "But a rabbit when you need something to chase."

He laughed through his nose, nuzzling me. "*My* little rabbit," he reminded, feathering his lips against mine. "And my wolf, too."

A low whistle interrupted the moment. Adam leaned back,

glancing toward the two bystanders who were rooted in place. Their mouths popped open, their eyes distended.

There was no mistaking the bloating in their pants, either.

"Show's over." Adam warned, jerking his head to the gallery entrance. "Leave or I bury you. Your choice."

I wouldn't put it past him, either.

"Jesus," the shorter of the two said, reaching for his buddy, heaving him in his direction.

"Was that Adam Ryan?" he asked.

We never heard his response.

Adam slid out of me, the plug of his cock releasing thick ropes of his cum dribbling over my swollen lower lips. "Shit," he mumbled, his face a slate of sheepishness and pride. He scratched at the back of his neck, staring at the mess. "I didn't think that through."

Bullshit. He was proud of himself.

"Do you ever?" I questioned with a laugh, lifting a brow.

Adam pondered it for a beat of a second, his lips twitching with the formation of a cocky smile. "When it comes to you?" He slid a hand between us, mischief glowing in his eyes as he collected his cum with two of his fingers. His digits crowned my sensitive entrance, and my eyes fluttered shut as he fed them inside me, burying himself to the knuckles. "Never."

"It's not happening," I warned, expelling a breath as he curved his fingers inside of me for good measure. I tried to conjure up a glare but all he did was take in the hitching of my chest and he knew this conversation was as good as done.

He could shove his cum back inside of me all he wanted; we had a deal. I finished school first, then we had a conversation. Until then, I was putting all our family planning trust in Tri-Cyclen. But there was fine print in that deal, a clause he held onto with the tenacity of Maria.

If for some reason big pharma failed me and it happened… then it happened.

Something told me if he knocked me up once, he'd want to keep making it happen again and again, no matter what my two-kid maximum-limit stipulation said.

He sized me up appreciatively, his eyes lingering on the smooth expanse of my stomach. "It might," he murmured, withdrawing his fingers. He adjusted my underwear to trap his cum with the other hand, the band snapping against the juncture of my thigh. My mouth opened to accept his fingers, my cheeks hollowing out as I sucked them clean for him, my brows bending in the middle.

Releasing him with a pop, I scowled up at him, blowing a breath up into my bangs. "Don't be so arrogant."

"I'm not arrogant, baby. I'm in love." He shrugged his shoulders. "Is it so wrong I want the world to know it?"

The blush spread from my chest right up to the apples of my cheeks. I rolled my eyes, failing to find an argument. With the ruddiness burning my body, I shifted my dress back into place.

"You should write for Hallmark." I could imagine the plotline already. *City girl moves to eerie small town and marries notorious criminal who fantasizes about getting her pregnant three times a day.*

"We're too X-rated for Hallmark." Adam slung an arm over my shoulder, his chuckle dark and predatory. "We make our own network."

I couldn't help it; I snorted out a laugh.

If he had it his way, I'd be pregnant tomorrow.

I wasn't sure that would be the worst thing to happen to me, either.

CHAPTER SEVEN

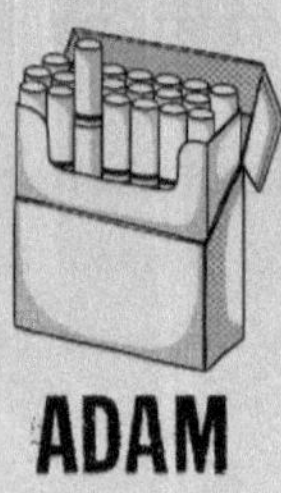

ADAM

"Where are you going?" Katrina mumbled into her pillow, her voice groggy and breathy with sleep. She slid an impatient hand out for me in bed, flitting her fingers, her eyes still closed.

I snatched my hoodie from the floor, bringing it to my nose for a sniff test, considering what story I was going to feed her. I could be as stealthy and quiet as I wanted, but there was no getting anything by her anymore. She had the situational awareness of someone who had a shit ton of trauma under her belt and was married to yours truly. My brothers had conditioned her to always be on alert and to never let her guard down, and I'd had a lifetime of being up to no good.

Tactical might as well have been her middle name.

I fed my arms through my hoodie and tugged my head through the opening. Adjusting the shock of messy strands on top of my head, I reached for the ball cap on my end table, fitting it over my head, tugging it down as far as it could go.

Where was I going…

Crawling onto the mattress, the springs squeaked in protest as I sidled up next to her in the dark. The strip of moonlight coming from the part of our curtains splayed across her pale skin, making her glow. "Go back to sleep," I urged, keeping my tone casual, pressing my lips to her temple. Her soft sigh warmed my chest, and I stroked her orange hair out behind her, running my fingers along her bare shoulder, tracing upward along the column of her neck, finally cradling her cheek. "I'm gonna go grab smokes."

There we go. Smokes. Thank you, post-nut clarity.

"There's an extra carton in the hallway credenza drawer," she whispered, turning her face into my palm, her lips feathering against my callused palm. "Stay."

"I smoked those," I lied.

"What?" She opened one eye, searching my face. Her makeup had smudged around her eyes and she had peeled the strip of her false lashes off her lash line after we'd gotten in. The pile looked closer to a dead spider on her end table near her phone and reusable water bottle. "When?"

I scratched at the scruff on my cheek, buying myself time by feigning a shitty memory. Katrina shifted the blanket, opening it for me, flashing me her naked body. I admired the series of love bites adorning her skin, the broken blood vessels in various stages of healing against her creamy complexion. Her pierced nipples pebbled to pretty points, courtesy of the draft she'd created with her motion, goosebumps stretching across her skin. My drained balls had the audacity to send a signal to my dick, blood gathering there once more.

Any other time, I would have slid back into bed with her, no argument necessary.

Except I had something I had to do that couldn't wait.

Something that had been bothering me since we left the museum.

When I didn't accept her invitation, my wife made a sound of protest. "Don't leave," she complained, patting the empty warm spot behind her where I really wanted to be. "Quit smoking."

I chuckled, lifting a brow at her sleepy form. "Are you telling me you're going to let me put a baby inside of you, then?"

That was also part of our deal.

Her dad died of cancer when she was ten and it had changed her family's lives irrevocably. Her older brother Sean had been forced to fill shoes he'd never wanted to fill to support his sisters and ma. It tore them apart.

Katrina didn't want to have kids if I was going to emulate behaviors that were so reminiscent to her dad and I couldn't fault her for that.

She deserved better, and so did whatever kids we had. So while I thought about knocking her up regularly, the conversation was tabled until she finished school.

Which gave me enough time to become the smoking cessation spokesperson.

Defeat swept over her pretty features, and she sighed, releasing the blanket, rolling over and giving me her bony back. The sheets had bunched at her waist, and she tugged the flat sheet to her chin.

I kissed her bare shoulder. "I'll be right back."

"And I'll be asleep."

"It's…" I glanced in the direction of the alarm clock on the dresser, craning my head behind the pile of her clothes. "Nine forty-five."

Katrina was a night owl, and it was normally me trying to pull her away from whatever held her attention and telling her to come to bed.

"I'm tired and sore," she mumbled, yawning. "You fucked me twice when we got home."

Precisely the intention. Tire her out long enough for her to fall asleep so I could slip out of the house. I'd taken advantage of my sister working a shift at the drugstore tonight and forced my wife onto her hands and knees on the first three steps of our stairs, the riser biting into her hips while I drove myself inside of her. When she still seemed too alert, I took her once more in our bedroom just for good measure with the tip of a knife pressed against her chin until blood beaded there. I lapped away at the copper offering with my tongue while she came around my cock, her face contorting with pain and pleasure while she chanted, *"No more. I can't handle any more."*

Good. The endorphins and adrenaline crash meant the third fuck was the charm.

"I'll be back," I assured, the mattress creaking as I stood upright.

"Bring me back Sour Patch Kids."

Of course, she was asking for candy. Her sweet tooth was unparalleled. We were within five feet of an empty box of Milk Duds and an open package of Skittles. Candy doubled as caffeine and melatonin to my wife. "I thought you said you'd be asleep."

"Second wind," she retorted around a yawn. "Quick power nap before I watch *True Blood*."

Gritting my teeth, I plodded to the door, grousing inwardly. Fucking Eric Northman.

Dipping out of our bedroom, I shut the door behind me, passing my sister's darkened bedroom, catching the silhouette of her college textbooks piled high on her desk. Saoirse was going to be a great doctor. I just wished there was more I could do, so she didn't have to bleed herself of all her energy to make it happen.

While she'd never blame me for our parents' dying before their time or the lengths I'd gone to retaliate, I knew some small part of her wondered how different our lives would be if I hadn't done what I did. If I could have just let it go.

But I couldn't let that go any more than I could the events of tonight. Katrina was too nosy on a good day, and I didn't trust she wouldn't demand to come if she knew what I was up to. I needed to do this on my own. I didn't want to chance her getting caught with me or running into Mr. Tortured Artist when she inevitably wandered off on her own. Telling her to do anything was akin to trying to reason with a wasp not to sting you when you swatted it away.

Katrina was disobedient to a fault and curious. She did what she wanted, when she wanted.

Besides, I preferred collecting ammunition to use against people on my terms. It was better if she slept through this one. I'd get her up to speed if I needed to.

I hoped I didn't need to.

"He blinked at me, Adam."

Truth was, I hadn't been able to get her words out of my head since she uttered them, no matter how skeptical I'd wanted to remain.

Even as I had led her out of the gallery room and taken one final look at the Founding Fathers, my attention lingered on the placard.

Something was off about the display, and it wasn't just because of what Katrina said.

Wagner had the artist's curse of perfectionism. He wouldn't model the Founding Fathers as a duo rather than a quintet unless it was on purpose.

Especially because the lineage of the Founding Fathers hadn't died in the seventeenth century. Their family name lived on in this town, used as currency to get what they wanted, when they wanted it.

Rhys had snubbed their forefathers, and he wasn't sparing any illusion that it was under the guise of "coming soon".

So why wasn't anyone talking about it?

There wasn't a drop sheet to thwart guests from looking at the pieces prematurely or a barricade to prevent them from entering the gallery room.

The muscles in my body tensed as I struggled to connect the dots with the information I had at my disposal. But then it hit me like a derailing train, sick understanding registering in my bones.

He *wanted* people to see.

It was intentional. A silent statement disguised as art. A message.

Who was I kidding? It wasn't a message at all. It was a warning, as sharp and ear piercing as a nuclear power plant meltdown.

I knew exactly who he directed it at. I'd bet my left nut that Vince could confirm it, too, if the asshole would deign to respond to my text message, that was.

My phone was burning a hole in my pocket as I left the house with Katrina's car keys and my wallet in tow, making a run for it to her Jeep in the rain, my unanswered text to Vince ping-ponging in my head. I didn't like it when Vince was quiet.

Quiet meant trouble. And trouble and Vince were dangerous in the same sentence.

What did you and Wagner talk about?

If there had been anyone who despised Rhys more than me, it was Vince. Their unaddressed rivalry went on for years. Their aesthetics shared similarities. Both looked and dressed like they'd walked off the set of a Tim Burton film. And for a time, they'd fucked the same girls— Vince out of spite, Rhys for good measure.

What ultimately separated them was Rhys executed quiet and broody perfectly, while Vince gave The Dobler-Dahmer Theory credence.

They didn't like each other. Never had, never would. So what business did they have together? What would ever compel him to meet with Rhys one-on-one without me, Max, or Gabe present?

My brothers and I had our version of secrets, sure. Max pretended it didn't bother him that his mother was a gold-digging whore who swapped husbands like their housekeepers changed bedsheets when her latest husband tired of her and her bullshit.

Gabe acted unaffected that his father was an abusive, overly religious zealot who hated him for reasons unknown.

Vince would never admit that his mother leaving him with his uncle had destroyed any chance of him growing up to be a half-decent human being. The mommy issues coupled by the gaping, festering abandonment wound, put him on the fast-track to becoming the future feature of a true crime podcast in the next five years tops.

There were some things among us that were unspoken but understood. We didn't keep things from one another because you never knew when one of us had to finish what the other had started.

That was how our family operated.

The trip to the museum was less than an eight-minute drive, and I parked at the end of the one-way street, clambering out of the Jeep. Employees were pouring out of the museum, and I tugged my hood over my ball cap, keeping my head down low. Josie was still right where I'd seen her last, her head bent, her lips moving as she balanced her till.

The sky had cracked open on the way home earlier, sheets of rain pelting the earth, and my footfalls echoing against the wet pavement in the poorly lit alleyway. A flickering light illuminated a short set of metal steps leading to the back door, and I took them two at a time. The handle on the back of the museum door gave easily, the must and dust of the museum filling my sinuses when I stepped inside, closing the door quietly behind me. I didn't want to alarm anyone I was in here. Darting down the narrow hallway, the thin carpet absorbed my strides. I was on a mission—get upstairs undetected.

The museum was eerily silent compared to the earlier thrum of music and revelry. I paused near the staff room, sloping forward and spotting what I assumed remained of the staff with their backs turned to me, deep in conversation. Timing their motions, I sprinted past the door quickly, dipping in the direction of the back of the museum.

I couldn't chance taking the main stairs. If the rumors were true, there was a secondary set of stairs somewhere in here, likely constructed for servants to remain out of sight, hundreds of years ago.

I strode through the first corridor on my left. The old electrical wiring on the sconce lighting created a trembling effect in the bulb, casting shadows along the oak wood wainscoting. The hall stretched for what felt like forever, and when I came to the end of it, I spun on the ball of my foot, appraising the passage.

I'd missed something. The right side of the hall was an exterior wall, which meant if there was a staircase, it had to be on the left side. Ambulating at a zombie's pace, I stretched my left arm out, applying pressure to the wall as I walked. The wainscotting glided under the calluses of my hands as I moved, nothing evidently amiss.

Shit. Did I have the wrong hallway? I considered the alternatives when the panel under my hand buckled and creaked unexpectedly, stilling me.

Bingo.

Pushing down harder on the panel, the hinges gave way; the wall swinging outward. I lifted my head, studying the curved stone staircase, the walls completely encased in slabs of gray stone. Fishing my phone out of my pocket, I turned on the flashlight feature and shut the panel door as quietly behind me as possible. When I heard the latch engage, I made my ascent up the stairs, using the tiny strobe of light to guide my way. If I thought the museum smelled stale, it was nothing compared to the tight confines of the hidden stairwell. Dust clung to the railing, and I could practically taste the cobwebs in my mouth as I made my ascent.

My phone vibrated in my hand, and I paused, glancing at my wife's text.

> Where are you? It doesn't take that long to grab smokes.

Her nap was short-lived. I considered not replying, but knowing she'd chain call me until I answered, I thumbed out a quick response.

> They didn't have Sour Patch Kids. Slight detour.

> You're full of shit.

I might as well pick out my funeral plot because she was gonna kill me. On cue, her contact ID illuminated my screen as her phone call rolled in. Her toothy grin as she posed in her wedding dress, with a bouquet of my ma's peonies and wisps of lavender bound with twine held in her hands. Her contentment in the picture contradicted what I knew would be her irritation on the other line.

I hit the decline button. "Sorry, Little Rabbit."

My insolence earned me another text message.

> Did you just screen my call?

As another phone call came in, I ignored the vibrations. I couldn't afford to burn precious time by arguing with her right now. I'd show her just how sorry I was later. If she wanted to hold a knife to my throat to change the power dynamic while I yielded, no problem.

Climbing the final riser, the outline of light silhouetting the door directed me. My fingers brushed against the lock and I drew my cheeks in, assessing it through shrewd eyes. It wasn't the first lock I picked and it wouldn't be the last, either. Testing the panel to determine what side the niche swung, I deduced it opened outward just like the door below.

Fishing the switchblade out of my pocket, the very one I'd used on Trina at home earlier, I pressed down on the release and the blade shot out; the whistle slicing through the air.

There.

Now it was like she was here with me when she inevitably found out where I'd been.

Nothing said romance like knives.

Placing my phone on the floor, the flashlight illuminated the cheap lock. I inserted the tip of the knife as deep as it could go into the lock's mouth, applying the slightest bit of pressure to jimmy the latch free. Rocking the tip back and forth, the click of the mechanisms disengaged. A pleased, expansive feeling filled my chest as I tugged on the loosened lock and fed it out of the latch. Pocketing it, my body slanted toward the door, and I listened carefully for sounds or movement beyond the door. Several minutes passed before I pushed on the door, the grit inside the hinges grating while tawny light filled the stairwell.

Wax figures greeted me. I was in the main gallery room.

This place was different in the light, but somehow, in the stiff quietude with motes of dust floating in the air and without the false sense of safety of the crowds, they were creepier, too.

More alert.

Shutting the door behind me, I made haste, my strides long as I took in the room, rushing to get myself directionally acquainted and recall the layout. We hadn't been here very long, but it was enough time for me to take a mental note of all the exits and rooms.

You never knew when you needed an escape route.

Sticking close to the walls, the collection of serial killers acted as my landmark, and knew I was close. The deeper into the inner sanctum of the museum I got, the more aware I grew of the sensation of every hair on my body standing upright with attention. An unmistakable prickling crawled up the back of my neck, addling my ability to think clearly.

I didn't scare easily. I had a history of intentionally doing things to provoke the Grim Reaper. But this place… it made me antsy.

'Cause some part of me knew, despite the absence of people, I wasn't alone.

Coming to a stop in the threshold of the Founding Father's gallery room, I pulled in a tight breath through my nose, fixing my stare at the Baroque-style ceiling, studying the artist's interpretation of the Rose of Rockchapel and the uncanny similarities she shared with Josephine Fischer.

"What the fuck are you up to?" I murmured under my breath, strolling into the room. I circled the Founding Fathers, taking in their details.

Unlike the other aged figures in the museum, the sheen of their wax gleamed, as though it hadn't had time to fully cure.

Rolling my shoulders out, I stepped toward Increase Walsh, engaging his beady blue eyes in a staring contest I wanted to lose.

"Blink, asshole," I commanded in a stilted voice. Frustration hardened my stomach, my muscles growing rigid as I straightened my spine.

Nothing.

The stale air stung my eyes, but I wasn't budging. I studied the minutiae, searching for an anomaly. I couldn't shake the thought that much like the Rose of Rockchapel above us, there was something familiar about this fucker, too. The whites of his eyes were too bright, almost human-like, complimented by the strain of red veins. My jaw screamed under my teeth as I lifted a hand, running the pad of my thumb along its lashes.

A chill worked its way down my spine at the contact. I'd expected the coarse feel of artificial hair, but they were soft.

Soft like human hair.

I rolled the knife still in my hand between my fingers. Fisting the shaft, I brought the tip of the blade to its chin, bringing myself nose to nose with him.

With little force, the blade sank into the first layer of wax, flaying away easily.

Too easily.

Withdrawing the knife, I reached out to touch the dust gathered at his chin, rubbing it between my fingers. It melted in the warmth of my fingers, leaving a greasy slip. I'd fucked around with enough lit candles and hot wax to know that wasn't supposed to happen with cured old wax.

This shit was fresh. Returning my focus to where my blade jutted, I applied more force. My tongue stabbed the inside of my cheek when the slow beading of blood spread under the layers of wax until I heard it.

The faintest suppressed cry, a panicked gurgle really in the back of a throat.

I stilled. What was the expression? It was the quiet ones you had to worry about?

"You crazy motherfucker," I announced under my breath.

I jerked the knife back, spots peppering my vision. Giving my head a shake, I closed my eyes, taking in a series of deep and controlled breaths.

What the fuck was going on here?

Opening my eyes, Increase's unmoving blue peepers tracked my motions. Another plea wrapped in a sob wrenched itself from deep in the back of his throat.

My pulse quickened in response. I ran the tip of the knife along the curtain of pale lashes, the glow from the sconce lighting glinting against the blade. Settling the knife under his lower lid, I brought my face closer to his, the tip of the blade scraping away at the thin wax, layer by layer, until I met human flesh.

"Blink or I'll gouge it out," I gritted out, my blood pressure surging. *"Pick."*

"I wouldn't do that," a familiar hoarse voice rasped behind me.

The man of the fucking hour. Tapering my eyes, I twisted on the ball of my Converse, taking him in. My shoulder blades tensed, and the laugh shot through my nose.

Rhys stood at the mouth of the gallery, shirtless. Rivulets of blood rolled down the slab of his pale chest, gliding down the long slope of his torso, settling in the grooves of his abdomen and the dusting of hair. For an artist, he had a body under those clothes, maybe from all the repetition of his motions when he was working. I'd give him that. Crimson speckled his face and arms, along with something else that looked a lot like bone shrapnel and chunks of sinew.

The slate of his expression remained impassive, his stony eyes bored while he wiped his face with the shirt bunched in his hand. All he did was smear the blood around like a monochromatic streak of paint.

"It would get messy fast," he tacked on, staring beyond me to Increase. Had he looked at himself in a mirror yet?

Clearly, he'd been busy. He looked like he'd gone to hell and won.

I directed the knife at the figure. "You put a person in there?"

Rhys was quiet for a beat of a moment, contemplating my question like it wasn't a straight yes or no answer. "The cruelest death is eternity."

He ran the back of his knuckles under his left cheekbone, staring down at his soiled hands. Sighing with displeasure, he tossed the shirt to the floor, pitching his hands on his waist.

"Who is that?" And were there others? I looked to Roberts, wondering if there was someone else in there, too.

He offered me an unreadable smile, licking at his stained lips. Rhys ambled closer, unhurried and content, coming to a stop near me. I kept my guard up, my grip flexing around the knife as I appraised him.

He had a good five inches over me, and he stretched his arms over his head, the knots in his back and shoulders clicking with the gesture. "They hurt her," he justified around a yawn, refusing to give me a straight answer. "It had to be done."

They hurt who?

But then it struck me with the force of a Category Five hurricane, knocking the air from my lungs. I glanced behind me, taking in those glacial blue eyes again.

I knew whose stare that was.

"You didn't," I murmured, failing to contain the approval from my voice.

"You'd do the same, wouldn't you? Regardless of their last name?" he asked, his timber calm. "If it was your wife." I stiffened at the mere mention of Katrina, my nostrils flaring with warning to select his next words carefully. "If you could kill what harmed her… wouldn't you?"

I lowered my arm holding the knife, my thumb playing along the dull spine.

Katrina's observation from earlier whirred in my head. *"They're together, aren't they?"*

"You're in love with her, aren't you?" My stare skated upward, snagging on the painting above me in her likeness. "Josephine Fischer. You're in love with her?"

"Love." He laughed through his nose.

Right. Love wasn't the right word for what people like him and I experienced.

It was deadlier than that.

Obsession.

The pieces of the puzzle came together. "Vince in on this?"

He sneered at the mention of my brother's name. "Markov is proving to be useful, yes."

I was going to need a lot more than that. Vince didn't help anyone for free.

Rhys sighed. "Don't look at me like you're a saint, Ryan. You've got a track record that precedes you."

"And?"

Rhys gave me what I thought was his version of a smile. Or a simper. I couldn't be sure. "*And*, you would understand better than anyone, just like Markov does. The law doesn't favor the likes of us. We don't look the part."

"You've got a squeaky-clean record," I informed him.

He regarded me through shrewd eyes, smiling. "And I intend to keep it that way with his help when I'm done."

I stared at the figures again; the words registering in my head. "The crematorium." So what the fuck did Vince want in exchange?

"For my tunnel access, yes."

I cursed inwardly. The tunnels.

There were a series of underpasses that ran beneath Rockchapel, hundreds of years old. The Founding Fathers had ordered their design in the event trouble happened upon them.

No one knew why or what they were running from, but I didn't think it was just the Witch Trials.

The town had ordered them to be sealed off fifty years ago.

Save for one, apparently.

"Why?" I questioned.

What the fuck could Vince possibly want with his access?

"I didn't care to ask."

"Do you normally invest all your trust in people you don't like?" Vince wasn't someone you trusted, not like that. He was as dependable as a king cobra.

"We're taking a chance on one another. Romantic, isn't it?"

He stepped closer to Increase, staring into the faces of his work. He closed a hand around his jaw, sneering down at him. "Don't cause me anymore trouble or I'm coming for your tongue next," he warned.

I could only guess what else he'd taken from him. "How are you keeping them alive?"

I didn't expect him to indulge me, but without meeting my eyes, he did.

"It's just the one," he said, before glancing at Roberts. "He didn't make it, and…" he looked down at himself, smiling a little, "well, we'll say the other two didn't fair all that well tonight, either."

But that meant there was still one remaining.

There was no way in hell he was going to get away with this.

You didn't just kill people in a small town and hope for the best, but he sure as fuck had picked the right person to help him.

Which meant it was only a matter of time before this shit ended up on my doorstep. "So, then?"

Rhys took a reluctant breath before tugging Increase's breeches down over the length of his glossy legs, revealing his how. A catheter ran from his wax-covered cock, secured with a piece of duct tape to his leg. The drainage tube fed into a collection bag further down his leg.

My stomach bottomed out when I stared at the dead space below his cock. He'd castrated him.

"He screamed," Rhys offered, following my line of sight. "But not as much as she did when they took her forcefully, I'm sure." His jaw turned to stone at his own observation. He tugged the figure's pants back up; the waistband slapping against the dull wax. Lifting the sleeve of his doublet up, the flexible tube protruded through another opening.

I hadn't been able to tell there was an IV in his hand because of the gloves. The pouch covertly tucked out of sight.

Rhys Wagner was fucking diabolical and psychotic, and I couldn't decide if it impressed me or not.

"Whose guts do you have all over you, Picasso?"

His stance widened, an irritated sigh escaping him. "You're chattier than I recall." Yeah, it came with being married to a motormouth. "And I think you mean Pollock."

Yeah, same shit. All artists were equal in nature—self-obsessed, perfectionist egomaniacs. Only thing that differentiated Rhys from them was the evidence that he was also a raging lunatic with a blood lust. "If I have to potentially clean up one of Vince's messes, I need the facts."

"Then the facts are as you see them." He kicked his chin toward the figures. "I did to them what you would have done and I intend to do what you *have* done." I tensed at his word choice.

We weren't the same. I didn't care how he wanted to position it.

"You're that fucking arrogant that you display your kills?" He really was a modern-day version of Ed Gein. They were borderline pieces of furniture with a pulse—or *had* been in Roberts' case.

"Display my kills," he pondered thoughtfully, examining invisible dirt under his fingernails with a cold, clinical calculation. "They're not displays." Those flinty eyes had the effect of a serrated blade slicing through me. "And they're not all dead. They're a promise to her." He rolled his neck back and forth. "A gift."

A gift.

I wasn't sure how responsive Josie would be to his version of gift giving. She struck me as the type who'd be happier with a book and content with being left the fuck alone, not dragged into whatever slasher film he was the villain in.

"Death is the only way any of us reclaim what we lost." He tipped his head back, his profile softening as he took in the ceiling. "That's why we do the things we do, Adam. We can't afford to hesitate. That's how we rewrite the narrative of who and what we are. And if I have to trap her here until I break her down and reshape her into who I know she is," he pulled in a deep, satisfying breath, "then I will."

Yep, totally fucking unhinged. But not entirely wrong, not that I'd ever tell him that.

"Go home," he advised, turning on his heel, declaring the conversation over by walking away. "I have something to take care of." His firm footfalls halted, his profile easy as he met my eyes over his shoulder. "This town owes us for its atrocities. We're exterminating the problems they've allowed to go unpunished because they had the right last names." As he crossed the gallery's entrance, he called out, his timber echoing, "And for fuck's sake, go out through the front doors."

I SLAMMED Katrina's car door closed behind me, letting my head fall back against my seat. My thumb ran along the teeth in the car key, my attention fixed straight ahead. I'd left through the front door like he'd asked, but I couldn't help but study the empty box office Josie had hidden behind all night.

Revenge. Rhys and I weren't that different.

Only I had done it for myself, for my parents—he'd done it all for her. And if I was right about who I thought I saw looking back at me behind the wax, her sister and what remained of her friends' numbers were up.

My phone pulsed in the cup holder where I'd deposited it, and I braced myself for the berating Katrina was going to give me.

But it wasn't her name on my phone. Irritation heated my body, and I jammed my finger against the answer button.

"Hi, honey," Vince taunted, the smile clear in his tone. "Looking for me?"

I scraped a palm over my face, blowing out a terse exhale. "You can't stay out of trouble, can you?"

I heard the working of a lighter on his end, and it ignited the craving for my own. Or six at this rate. "No more than you can, brother," he assured around the cigarette.

"Do you really want to be making deals with Rhys?"

Vince chuckled as though the whole thing was of no consequence. "The way I see it," he began, exhaling, and I could envision the hazy, cloud of smoke momentarily masking his sharp features as he blew the thick plumes out of his mouth with control. "Is that he has something I need."

I rested my arm against the lip of the door, my knuckles rapping against the cold window while I tracked a raindrop racing with another. "What do you want with the tunnels?"

"Wouldn't you rather find out?"

No, not really. "He's got people—*bodies*—trapped in those wax figures."

"*And*?" Vince stated like it was a nonissue.

"And Katrina's suspicious."

He let out a throaty, unsurprised laugh. "Christ, nothing gets by that one." He paused. "I suppose that's our fault."

The warmth of pride spread through my chest, the faintest hint of a smirk lifting my lips. "We taught her well."

My phone beeped with the warning of an incoming call. I peeled the phone from my cheek, grimacing at her name. "I gotta go. It's her."

"Adam," Vince said. "Not a word about the figures. She'll bust my balls."

I huffed, straightening in my seat. "So it's better she busts mine?"

"You know it won't just be the figures she'll want information on. She'll want to see the tunnels."

"*I* want to see the tunnels," I argued. What the fuck was down there? What did he want with the tunnels?

He hung up on me. "Fucking asshole." I accepted Katrina's call, reaching for the pack of cigarettes in the other cupholder. "Hey."

"Hey?" she questioned sarcastically. "I'm about thirty seconds from logging into your iCloud and using Find My iPhone."

"Baby—"

She ignored me, charging on, her volume rising. "This is shady as fuck, even for you. Who are you with?"

"No one." Rhys didn't count because I hadn't wanted to be with him anymore than someone wanted to discover they had an STD.

"Don't lie to me, Adam Ryan!" she shrieked. I winced, letting my head fall back against the headrest. We were in full name territory. Hell hath no fury like a little rabbit scorned. "If you come home smelling like some *bit*—"

"Are you fucking serious, Katrina?" I cut her off with a growl, pressing my fingers into my closed eyes to calm myself down. Like I had time or eyes for anyone else. But no matter how hard I fought to collect myself, hot lava spilled in my gut, igniting my entire body like gasoline. It scorched a violent path and forced my blood pressure to surge while my pulse raged in my ears. After *everything* we'd gone through, every fucking thing I'd done just to get her back, I'd never gamble losing her. No one compared to her. No one. "I have enough to eat at home. Why would I want anyone else but you?"

The stilted silence floated between us. She shuffled in bed, no doubt cradling her knees to her chest. "Then why won't you just tell me where you are?" she whispered.

Thinking better of wasting time lighting a cigarette, I sighed through my nose and glanced in my rearview mirror, finding the glow of the museum.

Sorry, Vince. He wanted to keep secrets. I wanted to keep my wife.

He could deal with her wrath.

Feeding the car key into the ignition, I turned the key over, and the engine hummed to life. "You were right." I sandwiched my phone between my shoulder and my ear, and tugged the shift into drive, listening to the audible, anxious shift of her breathing.

The sound had my cock stirring.

"I was right?" she inquired, faltering. She couldn't conceal her intrigue, though. Her insecurity over my absence faded. "About what?"

While the museum shrunk in my side mirror, the ominous choke-hold of the edifice, its countless victims, and the horrors it harbored, never left me.

"The wax figures." I licked my lips, catching the way she tried to control the excited gasp wrenching free from her lungs. "You were right."

TO BE CONTINUED...

AUTHOR'S NOTE

Thank you for reading *Scopaesthesia*, book #1.5 in the In Secret We Sin series! Want more of Katrina and Adam?

Read *Adrenaline*, book one in the series now!

Four years ago, I betrayed his trust.
He retaliated by breaking my heart.
Adam Ryan had secrets.
The kind better off where they belonged.
Buried.
As an urban explorer, I'm not afraid of a little trouble.
But when I venture to the one place Adam forbade me from, I get more
than I bargained for.
Him and his friends.
Along with their threats.
Their violence.
And their lust.
Adam might claim to still hate me.
What he hates more?
That his friends want me, too.
But they're not the only threat to my existence.
Someone else is after me.
Someone who knows Adam's secrets as well as they know mine.

ABOUT THE AUTHOR

A.L. Woods is a bestselling author of roller coaster romances, caffeine aficionado, and collector of Sailor Moon paraphernalia.

She lives 40 minutes west of Toronto, Ontario with her partner, Michael, and their 8lb larger-than-life miniature dachshund, Maia.

She believes that burritos should be in their own food group, loves the fall, winged liner, and listening to metalcore at an offensive level.

For photographic evidence of her shenanigans, or cute photos of Maia, follow her on social media.

Website: https://amandawrites.ca/

Be sure to subscribe to her newsletter on her website so you don't miss out on exclusive content!

instagram.com/amandalwrites

facebook.com/AmandaLWrites

tiktok.com/@amandalwrites

bookbub.com/authors/a-l-woods-78fa07fa-3ae1-485f-a058-e794a97bfcf1